DANCING THROUGH LIFE

BOOK ONE

Dancing
ON A
HIGH WIRE

PATRICIA M. ROBERTSON

Chapter 1

She felt like she had been punched in the stomach. Nausea, dizziness, swept over her.

"I have to sit down."

"You are already sitting down," a voice gently stated.

"Then I have to stand up, do something," she said but she remained sitting.

"Sara, talk to me. Are you okay?" the young man asked.

"I'm not okay. I gotta get out of here. I have to go home." A ray of sunlight slipped through the window onto the table. How could it be sunny, she asked herself?

"You are home, Sara. This is your apartment."

"Oh," she said as she looked around. Nothing looked familiar. Nothing seemed real. It didn't seem possible. This couldn't be her home. Nothing looked the same.

"Then you better go," she told the man sitting next to her.

"Not till I know you are okay."

"I'm not okay, but you have to go. Please go. I can't deal with this now."

"Okay, if you say so," he reluctantly got up and started for the door then turned back to look at her. "Call me, or I'll call you later, okay?"

Sara didn't respond as he let himself out the door.

"What has just happened?" she asked herself as she sat, the nausea giving way to numbness. This couldn't be real. Couldn't be happening to her. She had her whole life ahead of her, a life she had planned out, a life she had been going to share with Jeff. Now that was all gone.

Was it only yesterday that she had been in love? Two students at Michigan State University, young and in love. She remembered ...

"Hi ya, sweetheart," the lanky young man snuck up behind the petite figure sitting on a stone bench and staring intensely beyond the book in her lap, across the expanse of green grass behind the administration building and sloping down to the rapids of the Red Cedar River. Across the concrete steps on the neighboring shore were fat ducks sleeping in the sun. Across the expanse of campus the bright spring sky was broken only by the outline of white clouds. In one fell swoop, Jeff engulfed her from behind into a giant bear hug that knocked the book off her lap and onto the sidewalk and almost lifted her bodily off the bench.

"Jeff, what are you doing?"

Jeff continued to hold her in his bear hug, resting his head on her head with a wild toothy grin and rocking gently back and forth, his arms clasped firmly together under her full breasts.

"You're crazy. Let me go. People are staring."

"So let them stare."

"You're impossible," Sara said with a true note of frustration but inside she loved it, loved the feel of his nearness towering above her. She loved the strong arms around her waist, loved his impetuousness and his open displays of affection, so different from her own inhibitions. Somehow Jeff, with his warmth and enthusiasm, had broken through her tight space that kept others at a distance and had done it so genuinely that she had not felt offended. He wasn't like the other guys who invaded her space, tried to thrust themselves into her personal atmosphere, not because they liked her and respected her but because they wanted something from her. He gave his friendship and love so that she wanted to give to him in return. Because he made no demands she felt free to give, whatever she wanted to give, and both slowly and like a whirlwind he had zoomed into her life and won her over.

Theirs was an easy friendship, easy and natural. Not full of the silly hassles that seemed to beset the relationships of other couples they knew. They had met in the dorm and shared several of those general first-year courses that no one was allowed to escape. Together they went through all the frustrations and traumas of the first year at a mega-university. They both came from small towns USA, Michigan style, middle class families.

As Sara allowed herself to relax in Jeff's arms, Jeff let go and sidled up next to her on the bench. Sara felt both a feeling of relief from the embarrassment of being stared at by others, seeing two people so obviously in love, but also a sense of disappointment at having the warmth of his arms removed from her.

"You love it and you know it," Jeff remarked as he sat next to her.

Sara had to smile, "I love you, not everything you do. Look what you did to my book, all my notes have been scattered all over and I've lost my place."

"You weren't really studying anyway."

"What do you mean I wasn't studying, how do you know?" Sara enjoyed fighting with Jeff, even when she knew he was right and she was just being stubborn. Jeff knew it too. He enjoyed their little verbal repartees. So far they had never had a real argument, a serious fight, just teasing and love spats.

Jeff stared at Sara with his big impetuous grin. Sara couldn't resist his smile, yet because of that she felt she had to withstand his attraction.

"Stop smiling at me like that. I'm serious." Jeff just continued to grin. "And I was too studying. I've been going over some of these pictures of paintings by early impressionists and studying their style. I'm thinking I might do a series of paintings imitating their techniques and try to incorporate them into my own style, or something like that," Sara lied. Jeff just grinned, further confusing her.

"And then you know, I've been studying that time period, trying to put it into perspective with the painters of the times, their lifestyles, and how that influenced their paintings . . . Darn, will you please stop staring at me like that.

"But I like to stare at you."

"Just stop it," Sara was starting to get angry. "All right, have it your way. You can sit there and grin all day if you want. I'm leaving." Sara closed her book and prepared to leave. She took one last look at Jeff before making her move, not really wanting to leave. Jeff was still grinning. He loved it when she was angry like that.

"I was just thinking," he said and paused. "I was just thinking, we ought to discuss what we're going to do in the future."

"What are you talking about?"

Jeff became suddenly serious. "Our future, together, you know."

"No, I don't know." She paused before adding, "You're not talking about marriage, are you?"

"Why not? We'll be seniors soon, and then graduates, why not do this together, plan a life together."

"Marriage, you and me?"

"It would be difficult to do so alone."

"Jeff, I . . ." She didn't know what to say. They were still so young, he was so impetuous. And what about a career? And yet Jeff was so supportive of her art, what better person to have by her side while she built a career?

"But we're both so young."

"More time for us to be together. We aren't teenagers any more. If we get married now we have a better chance of making it sixty years."

"What about our parents?"

"Mine love you as much as I do."

"It's so soon, so impulsive . . ." So unlike her, she thought, she who was always so careful, who liked a plan despite her artistic side. It wasn't exactly her dream proposal and yet ... here he was, her dream man. She couldn't imagine finding anyone she loved more. She looked across the expanse of lawn and river to the opposite side as she pondered the question, avoiding his gaze. How could she say no?

"Yes," she finally said, much to Jeff's relief.

"I knew you would say yes if I kept asking," Jeff said as he picked her up and planted a kiss on her lips. "Let's celebrate."

That had been last spring. What had happened since then to lead to this? It was just yesterday, just this morning that she still had that illusion of love. Now it was gone. Would it ever return? Popped by one phrase, the bubble that had been her life had exploded. What would she do now?

Her roommate found her at the kitchen table, still sitting where Jeff had left her that morning.

"Sara, are you okay?"

Sara appreciated the concern in her voice but it seemed to be spoken through a tunnel.

"Sara," Anne repeated, finally breaking through to whatever place she had retreated.

4

Sara looked up, "Oh, hi, when did you get here?"

"Jeff called me. He told me what happened. Are you okay?"

"Sure, yeah, I'm fine. I'm okay," Sara repeated.

"You don't look okay."

"No, I'm fine, just fine. I just need a little fresh air, yes, fresh air will help," she said and proceeded to try to stand up only to have her legs buckle underneath her as her head swam. Anne stepped in beside her to help hold her up.

"Here, let me help you. Let's get you to a more comfortable seat." She helped Sara edge her way to the couch, slipped her into her favorite spot and wrapped a blanket around her.

"You just sit there. I'm going to fix you some tea. Sit back. I'll take care of everything. Everything is going to be okay," Anne assured her. Sara knew she was wrong.

Chapter 2

"There's no easy way to say this. We are changing our food services from our own program to another provider. We expect to save well over thirty thousand dollars by doing this. It will mean some changes in staffing, but I want to assure you that you will have the opportunity to apply for positions with the new provider," the executive director informed them at the mandatory employee meeting for food service workers.

When she had first heard about the meeting she hadn't been concerned. Probably some more minor policy changes. Seemed someone was always coming up with changes. Every time they got a new executive director, that director had to make a mark by introducing changes, whether warranted or not. There had been some rumblings, always were rumblings and rumors in any organization where there were people, so this one was no exception. At times there had been talk of unionizing, but overall, she had been happy with management and saw no reason for a union. She had already outlasted four executive directors. She knew the drill. She figured she would outlast this one as well.

She had started working at the retirement community part-time out of high school, left when she had her babies then began working again for over twenty-five years once her youngest started grade school. She was one of the old-timers. As such she had the first option at the check-in desk where she could sit and rest her feet, but she didn't always take that option, enjoying waiting on the residents who had become friends over the years. They had become like family. She enjoyed her job, enjoyed the people she worked with and for, and looked forward to working there for another ten years until she was ready to retire.

She had heard it all before but this time was different. She tried to ignore the tension forming in her shoulders and the unsettled feeling in her stomach as he went on to introduce the management staff for the new company. Her boss would have the opportunity for a management position with the company at another site. Everyone else would have a month probationary period as they decided who would stay and who would go. They were told not to say anything to the residents until they were told about the change at the meeting that afternoon.

"What do you think?" one of her co-workers asked as they walked out of the meeting together.

"I don't know what to think. It's too soon to tell."

"I don't know about you but I'm going to start looking for another job. I can't afford to be without work," another said.

"At least my husband still has his job. It will be hard if I lose this job, but not impossible. But what will you do, Esther? You still have kids at home."

"I guess I'll worry about it when it happens. Maybe it won't be so bad."

"Let's hope so," Margaret said as they went to their cars.

Esther didn't know what to think. After all, she had lasted for twenty-five years; she figured she could make it another five to ten years. Still she felt dizzy, unsure of herself; her legs were like lead weights as she walked to her car.

Chapter 3

Sara woke up after a hard sleep. She felt strangely calm. It had all been a dream, a bad dream, she told herself. In her dream, Jeff had broken off their engagement. In her dream he had told her he was gay. Couldn't possibly be true. What a nightmare. Today she would get up and go to class, then go to work and she would see Jeff at lunch as they always met for lunch and she would tell him about her dream and they would both laugh. And then the world would be right again. She just had to get through the morning until she could see him.

She got out of bed, took a quick shower, dressed and prepared to leave for her eight o'clock class.

"You up," Anne asked

"No, I'm sleep walking. What do you think I'm doing? I've got my eight o'clock. Can't sleep through that."

"I thought after yesterday that maybe you wouldn't go to class."

"Why wouldn't I go to class?"

"Because, you know," Anne hesitated, unsure how much to say, "After your break-up."

"No, that was just a bad dream. I just need to talk to Jeff and everything will be fine."

"No, Sara, it wasn't a dream, it was real. Remember?"

"No, it was all a mistake. Just wait till I talk to Jeff. Now I have to go to class," Sara stated as she pulled on her coat.

Anne walked over and gently put her hand on Sara's arm. "No, Sara, it's true." Sara pulled away, finished putting her coat on and walked out the door.

"No, it's not true, and if you were a good friend you would let me go."

Sara sailed through her eight o'clock class and worked her three-hour shift at the book store as if nothing had happened. She met Jeff at the Union grill, same as she had every Wednesday for the past two years, as long as their work and class schedule allowed.

Jeff seemed surprised to see her.

"I wasn't sure you would show up."

"Why wouldn't I? It's Wednesday, isn't it?"

"Yes, but after yesterday I wasn't sure you would want to see me."

"Why wouldn't I want to see my fiancé?"

"Sara, remember? Yesterday? We can't get married."

"Oh, that, that was just a mistake. I'm sure you're mistaken."

"No, Sara, I'm not. I'm gay. I've struggled with this for years. I've only just recently found the strength to admit who I am."

"But how do you know? How can you be sure? This is just a bad dream. This can't be happening to me."

"This isn't just about you, you know. It's happening to me, too. I didn't exactly choose this."

"Yes, you did, you chose . . ." Sara struggled to find the words, "You chose 'this' over me, over all we shared. How can you do this?"

"No, I didn't choose this. I didn't want this, tried to avoid it for years but I can't lie to myself anymore. And I can't continue to lie to you."

"But what about all of our plans? I thought you loved me."

"I do love you, just not in the way that you want."

"Then why did you propose? Why did you go out with me?"

"Maybe because I just wasn't ready to accept the truth back then. I do love you, if I were to marry any woman, it would be you." Jeff paused to allow what he was saying to sink in. When Sara didn't respond he continued, reaching for her hand, "I know it's hard. I'm hoping we can still be friends. Just think how hard this has been for me?"

"You don't get to decide whether we can be friends or not." Sara pulled her hand away. "You're the one who broke up with me, remember. I think you better go." Sara didn't know what to say. She had been so sure it was a mistake, a cruel mistake, but here was Jeff again, saying the same terrible things he had said yesterday so maybe it was true. But it couldn't be true.

Sara stared down at the salad untouched on her tray. "If you don't leave, I guess I will."

"No, don't get up, Sara, I'm going," Jeff said as he left.

Sara called Anne. She didn't wait for Anne to say hello before saying, "Anne, Jeff and I are broke up."

"I know, Sara, Where are you?"

"At the Union."

"I'll be right there," Anne said and hung up.

Sara's salad remained untouched when Anne found her.

"I can't believe it. It wasn't a bad dream," Sara told her.

"I know. Let's get out of here."

"He couldn't be gay, could he? I would have known, should have known. How could I have been dating someone for two years and not know?" she said as she left with Anne.

Chapter 4

Sara existed in a cocoon of numbness for weeks after the break-up. It helped her keep moving as friends kept asking her if she was okay. She focused on her classes and work. Fortunately they had not set a date yet, wanting to graduate and get jobs first before planning a wedding so there was no church or hall to cancel. It was her senior year. She had her senior project to complete, which occupied most of her attention. She dreaded the Christmas holidays. Thanksgiving had been a disaster.

"So where is that young man of yours?" her grandmother asked upon arrival. "When do we get to meet him?"

Her mom had intervened, taking her grandmother's coat and telling her, "They broke up, remember, I told you about it."

"No, you didn't. No one tells me anything," she replied.

"Yes, I did, you just forgot," her mother said with a tone that indicated no more was to be said.

Later, after dinner, while attempting to drown her sorrows in chocolate pecan pie, her aunt had commented, "If you want to get a man, you better stay away from those desserts."

Sara stopped with pie on her fork mid-way to her mouth.

"Don't you worry, honey," her uncle had interjected, "A man likes a woman with a little meat on her bones. Truth be told, a Rubenesque figure is better than a Twiggy," he said, referring to a model from his youth.

Sara put her fork down, no longer hungry, feeling the familiar churning in her stomach that had occurred repeatedly since the break-up.

The next day, while shopping, she had reluctantly gone into the dressing room with a dress her mother wanted her to try on. She stared at herself in the mirror, looking at the soft round contours of her body and thinking, "Fat, fat, fat, no wonder I can't get a man." She vowed to lose weight, after the holidays. She was relieved to finally escape back to her apartment, not that she was able to escape her worst critic, herself.

At least she had been able to avoid the "conversation" with her mom. It would be harder to do that over Christmas with so much more time. She had hoped to spend part of the holidays with Jeff at his parents. She liked his parents. They were so different from hers. His parents were teachers at a local college. His mom was supportive of Sara and her ambitions. Her own parents thought she was wasting her time with a degree in Art and Design.

"How are you going to make a living with that?" her ever practical dad kept asking.

"She'll just have to find a good man to support her," her mom was even worse. She couldn't believe that in this day and age her mom still thought a woman needed a man to be "fulfilled." Sara had been raised, somewhat sheltered from the world, homeschooled until high school, then attending a Christian high school. Her parents were evangelical fundamentalists, or so she found out when immersed in the secular world of college life.

Jeff was Catholic and had attended a Catholic high school. Her parents had been suspicious of him all along.

"Are Catholics even Christian?" her mom had asked when she first told her about him.

"Yes, mom. They are Christian. They believe Jesus is the Christ. We have more in common than you realize."

Sara had appreciated the fact that Jeff was religious, yet in a different way from her. She had been looking for something different and she found it in Jeff.

"It's probably for the best," her mom had said when she told them. "The faith differences were just too much. Now you can find a nice young man from our church. You are attending church while at college, aren't you?"

"Sure, mom. I've got to go," Sara hung up. How could she tell her parents Jeff was gay? It would be too much for them to absorb. Probably better left unsaid. Let them think what they want to think. Let them think it was the faith differences that had driven them apart.

She hadn't been entirely honest with her mom about attending church. She had been attending services at the non-denominational church at the college. She liked mixing with students from different faiths. Her first official date with Jeff had been attending a Thanksgiving service there, during their sophomore year. She remembered hanging out with him at the social hour after the service and thinking how fortunate she was to have found someone she could share her faith with, even if they came from different backgrounds. After that they started attending church together on a regular basis. She attended Jeff's church at times, other times Jeff attended her church.

Jeff had been so supportive of her art. In fact he had been her primary support in choosing studio art as a major her sophomore year when her more practical side had told her to go into teaching.

"And now, here I am, graduating with a useless degree, no job prospects and no husband," she thought to herself. "Why had I listened to him? I should have gone into elementary education with an Art minor, like my dad had wanted. Then I could have gotten a teaching job," she told herself, although she realized that in the current economy and poor job market, a teaching certificate was no guarantee of a job. Jeff had also encouraged her in design, learning computer design programs. Maybe she could get a job using those skills while pursuing her art on the side. She guessed she had him to thank for that.

So many of her friends were seriously dating or engaged. It seemed they had come for their "MRS" degree rather than a B.A. It was hard, feeling like she was being left behind once again. Just like in high school where she had struggled to fit in. And dates? They were few and far between. It had been so nice to have someone to go places with, to have a regular Friday and Saturday night date. Someone to meet for lunch, someone so she didn't have to go to parties alone. Jeff had been that someone for her. How would she get along without him? And New Year's once again without a date? How could she face that?

Chapter 5

"So how did it go with Sara?" Mike had been waiting for his call.

"I don't know. She seemed to be in shock. I'm not sure she heard me."

"Well, give her some time. After all, you've been thinking about this for years. She didn't know this was coming. You didn't come to this realization overnight. It may take her a while."

That he didn't, Jeff thought to himself as he hung up. He had been struggling all of his life, only he hadn't realized it until recently. He wasn't sure exactly when he had started to recognize that he was different from the other kids. Then in high school, doesn't every high school student feel like they are different even as they strive to fit in? It's the ordinary high school angst. He had been active in sports, football in the fall, baseball in the spring. He had never been good enough for the basketball team, but football reigned supreme at his school so it had been his entry into the "popular" crowd. He had had his share of dates but usually as part of a "group" date as he and members of the football team would go out together, hook-up with willing girls and share their exploits afterwards. Alcohol had flowed freely. Those exploits left him feeling lonely and out of place, wanting more. They just didn't satisfy a need in him.

Then he had met Sara. They had hit it off right away. He had thought, maybe she was the one. Maybe she could fill the emptiness inside, maybe with her he could forget the other urges, temptations he was experiencing. They hadn't been sexually intimate, Sara insisting they wait till marriage and he was okay with that. It took the pressure off of him. They were physically close, touching, kissing, giving each other back massages but nothing further. He found this surprisingly easy to do.

While with Sara, he forgot about other women and other men … Well, he hoped that once they were married he'd forget about that as well.

He had met Michael at the Catholic Student Parish on campus at one of their functions. Mike had come with his roommate Chris. Jeff had liked both of them immediately but had been surprised when he found out they were part of the Dignity group on campus, a support group for gays and lesbians. He had avoided them after that until his best friend from high school had come out to him.

"You're what?"

"I'm gay. I've been wanting to tell you for years. I just wasn't sure how you would take it," Doug had told him. He hadn't been sure how to take it. Their friendship, that had been so free and easy up to that moment, was suddenly filled with tension and awkwardness.

"I'm not sure what to say," Jeff said.

"I was hoping you'd say it was okay. That we are still friends."

"Yeah, I mean, yes, we are still friends, but are you sure?"

"Would I have said something if I wasn't sure? Are things going to be weird between us now?"

"No, no, I hope not. I just need to think about this."

"Sure, you do that," Doug said, preparing to give him a hug before he left, as had been their custom, then switching to a handshake.

"A manly handshake," Jeff said to himself. How many times had he and Dough slept in the same room, even sharing the same bed over the years. And he had not known? Impossible. But if Doug, what about him?

Chapter 6

She hadn't made the cut. Esther had tried her best but she couldn't keep up with the young people. One of the first changes had been to get rid of the check-in desk. In its place was a podium. No more sitting during the day. Everyone was to be standing and active all day. It had been hard on her back and feet. Still, she had thought she had a chance. She suspected her dismissal had had more to do with her seniority and pay rate than her ability, but she had no way to prove that so was forced to accept her dismissal. She had given it her best. Maybe it wouldn't be so bad. At least she was eligible for unemployment. She could collect unemployment while she figured out what to do next.

Esther sighed, some Christmas this would be, she thought as she sat down at the kitchen table. She felt like the ground was shifting underneath her, leaving her shaky and confused.

"What's up, grandma?" her oldest grandson asked. She had been raising Josh and his brother, Scott, since Josh had been four, when her daughter had left.

"Nothing, Josh, nothing you need worry about."

"Grandma, I know there's something wrong. I'm not a child, tell me." He definitely wasn't a child. At not quite fourteen, he was older than many twenty-year-olds.

"What's up, honey?" her father asked, coming in from the front room.

"Where's your walker? You know you are supposed to be using your walker," she scolded, hoping to deflect attention from herself to her dad.

"I can get along fine in the house without my walker. It's a nuisance anyway, always banging into things and snagging on the carpet."

"You know what the doctor said."

"Yeah, yeah, so what's wrong with you? You look terrible."

"Thanks."

"You know what I mean." She knew what he meant all right. She wished she could hide her fears and feelings from him, but it didn't work. Her face was an open book where he was concerned.

"I didn't make the cut."

"At work?"

"Yes, they aren't going to keep me on. Those youngsters can run circles around me."

"But how reliable will they be? And how long will they stay? They don't know the residents like you do."

"I know that, I just wish management knew it."

"They do. They realize it, I'm sure, but it's a lot cheaper to hire someone still in high school than to keep on an employee that has been there for twenty-five years who works full-time and receives health benefits. How else are they going to provide all the savings they claim they will be able to provide?"

"I know, the bottom line is money, it's always money." They had already discussed this numerous times over the last month so when the inevitable came, it wasn't a complete shock. Still, it was hard. At loss for words, her dad had re-iterated what they both already knew.

"Don't worry, grandma, I can help with my paper route," Josh joined the conversation.

"No, that money is for you to save for college." Esther had been talking to him about college for years, implanting into his brain the message, priming him to be the first in their family to attend. "You are not going to give that up."

"I can take a second route."

"And when will you find time for school work? No, don't worry about it. Your great grandpa and I will work this out, like we always have." She hadn't made it this far without hitting a number of speed bumps along the way, as well as some collisions. Losing her husband, Dale, at a young age had been a collision. He had died when the kids were four and two, much the same age as her daughter's two children had been when Kathleen had left them. Too much of a painful coincidence, Esther had thought at the time. Two more small children for her to raise without the benefit of a father. About the time she adopted Josh and Scott, Esther's dad had moved in, ostensibly to help with raising the pair, but also because living alone was no longer a good option for him since his wife, Esther's mother, had died the year before.

Too many losses, Esther had thought at the time. Life had given her way too many challenges to deal with. Sometimes she didn't think she would make it. The memory of her husband's love and support helped, but it didn't make up for the loss of his physical presence. But there was also new life, young life, as she was given a second chance at parenting, raising her grandchildren. At forty-five she still had some energy left to help her with this challenge. Now at fifty-five, she felt like she had nothing left, what energy she had a decade earlier had been drained by this latest challenge. Fortunately, the children were also older and needed, not less attention, but different attention. They still needed her involvement in their lives, but they no longer required as much physical labor, changing diapers, running after toddlers. They were old enough to help out some now. This was good as her dad was slowly losing functions and was starting to need more attention. They were able to help her with their great grand-dad at times.

A life of care-taking, she thought. When was someone going to take care of her? Not any time soon, she figured.

She was grateful that Dale Jr. had successfully navigated the transition to adulthood and was self-sufficient, married to a wonderful young woman. Dale's wife was a great mother to her grandchildren and a good wife to her son. Who could ask for more in a daughter-in-law?

Fortunately there had been life insurance after her husband's death. He had died on the job, a freak accident. He had worked for the local energy company, climbing poles, installing wires, trouble-shooting problems in the field. Perhaps that was another reason for her light-headedness, she wondered, fear from watching her husband climb high poles, supported only by a belt. She remembered getting dizzy just watching him.

"Be careful up there," she would admonish him each day before he left for work. He would laugh and dismiss her fears.

"You know I'm always careful," he said giving her kiss.

When the transformer registered trouble, it had been shut down, or so they had thought when sent to work on it. It had been a quick, relatively painless death, or so she had been told, as if that would ease her loss. Besides the insurance money there had been money from the company to help make up for the loss of the family breadwinner, but, of course, nothing could make up for the loss of Dale. Over thirty years later, she still missed him. She wondered if that was what was at the heart of Kathleen's rebellion and drug use. No one can replace a father in a girl's heart.

Her friends wondered why she never remarried. She wondered herself, but with two small children to raise and then two grandchildren, who had time for dating? And she couldn't bring just anybody into her home, not with children to consider. Maybe someday she would have time for that as well as all the other things in her life that she had never had time for. Maybe someday she would have time for herself. She could always dream.

She had used the money to pay off the mortgage on their three-bedroom home. She also put some aside in a trust for both children to pay for college for them. When Dale Jr. decided college wasn't for him, he used the money for a trade school to become a licensed plumber and eventually was able to start his own business with what was left of the money. When it became obvious that Kathleen would not be going to college and couldn't be trusted with the money, Esther changed the trust, putting it in Kathleen's children's names. Fortunately she had maintained control of the money so Kathleen was not able to get it and use it for drugs. The remainder of the money had paid the bills until the children were both in school and she got a job. Between that and Social Security payments for her children, they had gotten by.

That money was long gone, except for the money in trust for Josh and Scott.

Josh and Scott's mother had been another collision. They had been on a collision course ever since inception it seemed. Strong-willed had not been the word for it. Kathleen had always wanted to do everything her way.

"Don't worry," her pastor had assured her when Kathleen had been in her terrible twos. "The strong-willed ones, if they can be tamed, are the future leaders. They are the ones most likely to buck the system, take the lead rather than give into peer pressure."

"Or end up in jail," Dale had cracked. It had seemed funny at the time.

"Or that," Pastor Jim had laughed. And so Kathleen had ended up in jail. She had had to go her own way. It didn't help that she didn't have her father's strong hand to guide her. She had been pregnant at twenty-two, again at twenty-four, and in and out of jail by the time Josh was four. Twelve years for breaking and entering, another offense after multiple earlier charges for drug possession and uttering and publishing – writing fake checks. Kathleen had to learn the hard way. And yet God was good. She seemed to be getting her life together while in jail, drug-free and attending college classes at the state's expense. She had served seven years of her sentence and hoped to get out earlier than the twelve years for good behavior. She might end up being the first in their family to get a college degree, even if by an unorthodox means. Still a degree was a degree.

Her beautiful baby girl, Esther's heart ached each time she thought about her. Josh looked so much like his mother, was smart like her too, but in a good way. Kathleen always used her brain for trouble. Josh applied himself to his school work. Where Kathleen had used her brain to get ahead, in a negative way, dreaming up schemes to get rich without having to do the required work, Josh had a good work ethic. Esther was relieved at this. If he had been anything like his mother she didn't know what they would have done. And Scott, while he didn't have his brother's brains or work ethic, was as easy going as they come. He would be another builder, following her dad around the house as he did repairs, hanging out in her dad's workshop. As it was, they were both proving to be blessings in her old age, not that she considered herself old at fifty-five.

Their son, Dale Jr., had been as different as night from day from their daughter. Not anywhere as smart, he had been easily manipulated and mislead by his older sister until he learned to distance himself from her. It had been a painful lesson for all involved. It had hurt Esther to watch his wide-eyed adulation turn to distrust, yet she knew it was a necessary lesson. She suspected that it had hurt Kathleen as well, somewhere deep inside her where Esther had not been able to reach. Still she believed that there was a kernel of good in her child, waiting to grow to life.

Dale Jr. had been as stable as Kathleen had been unstable, taking after his father, rock solid, someone you could count on. He didn't excel in book learning but was good with his hands.

He had two children whom she adored, not more than Josh and Scott, but in a different way. It was different when you were raising your grandchild, being mother and grandmother rolled into one, not to mention, father as well, rather than just grandmother. She had to be disciplinarian for Josh and Scott; fortunately they didn't require a lot of discipline.

But if Dale Jr., took after his dad, who did Kathleen take after? Certainly not her. She didn't know where Kathleen got her IQ and will of steel.

"Just like your uncle Steve, my brother," her mother had commented once. When Esther tried to find out more about him, her mother always evaded the question.

"He was the black sheep of the family," she had finally told her. "Haven't heard from him since he left home at sixteen. As far as I know he is long gone," was all Esther had gotten out of her.

At least she knew where her wayward daughter was, safely tucked away in prison, out of harm's way, so to speak. If anyone had to be worried, it would be the other inmates as Kathleen always had a way of coming out on top, even in the worst situations. No, Esther didn't worry so much about her safety while in prison. It was almost a relief not having any more late night phone calls or worrying when or if her daughter would show up. Yes, there are worse things than jail. Now if only she would discover religion while in prison, develop some type of relationship with God, then all of her worries would be lightened. She would say this time in jail had been worth it.

"Josh, don't you have homework?" Esther wanted him out of the kitchen so she could talk freely with her dad.

"You're not going to get rid of me that easily," he replied. Josh knew the ruse.

"All right. What will it take to get you out of here so grandpa and I can talk?"

"Just that last piece of pie from dinner last night," he said with a grin.

"What's going on in here?" Scott joined the group.

"Is your homework done?" Esther asked.

"Yes, can I watch TV now?"

"Sure, and take your brother with you. Josh, you share that pie."

"Oh boy, pie!" Scott said as Josh pulled the last piece out of the refrigerator

"Hey, that's mine," her dad protested.

"Take it, go on. Dad, let them have it," Esther said feigning anger even as she smiled. Her dad just grumbled.

"How about ice cream? It's not much if I have to share it," Josh asked.

"Yes, you can have ice cream, now get out of here."

"So what are we going to do?" her dad asked once Josh and Scott left, lowering himself into a kitchen chair.

"I don't know," Esther replied, resting her forehead into her right hand. "I can file for unemployment. That will help. And with the holidays coming up, maybe I can get some part-time work at a store."

"But what will you do for health benefits? Josh and Scott can get coverage through MIchild, I've got Medicare. You can't go without health care."

"COBRA is so expensive. It will take more than half of my unemployment to pay for it. I guess I'll have to go on-line and take my chances getting health care. Since I'm not working, I've got plenty of time to waste trying to get through," she said. "Hopefully I will qualify for a subsidy, being unemployed and all. Or maybe I'll just have to not get sick and go without for-awhile."

"No, you can't do that. Don't worry. Something will turn up."

"I know, it always does," Esther agreed, but why did God always have to take so long? Yesterday would have been none too soon for her. She felt every bit of her fifty-five years. She was too young to retire, too old to compete with people half her age. She didn't know if she would ever be able to retire. Her family counted on her income. She was the only one gainfully employed. They couldn't live on her dad's Social Security, would never consider it. That was for him. She knew he wanted to help though. One night last week she had come home and surprised him lifting weights and doing the exercises he had given up on a year ago.

"What are you doing?"

"Getting back in shape. Time for me to come out of retirement."

"What are you talking about?"

"We can't have both of us on the government dole. It's time I start pulling my weight around here."

"Like you haven't been pulling your weight. You've been so much help with Josh and Scott, watching them so I could work. And what about all those years raising us kids, like that wasn't pulling your weight."

"That was then, this is now. I've still got some good years in me."

"And I want you to be able to enjoy them. I appreciate the thought but I'll take care of everything. Besides I haven't lost my job just yet." That had been last week when she still had hope of keeping her job. This was this week, the ax had fallen.

"I'll be able to get something," she assured her dad. "They need people to give out food samples at Sam's Club on the weekends. Some of the other people who were let go are doing this. They told me about it. It's not a lot, but it will be something. I'll apply first thing tomorrow, right after I apply for unemployment. It will help us get through the holidays, and who knows, maybe it will lead to a real job with benefits."

"At Sam's," her dad laughed, "fat chance."

"At least it will be a start until something better comes along. We'll get by."

Chapter 7

Christmas went by without too much fanfare. Sara had managed to come back to East Lansing two days after Christmas, insisting she needed the time to work on her senior project and that she had plans for New Year's Eve. In actuality the plans were a bottle of wine, popcorn and a rented video, but she wasn't going to let her mom know that.

She hadn't been able to entirely avoid a "heart-to-heart" talk with her mom. Christmas Eve and Christmas Day had been filled with family. With her brothers and their families and her sister Joy and her husband and two children coming and going as they made the rounds between in-laws, the house had been in non-stop commotion. When Joy announced that she was pregnant again, it took the attention off of her, to her relief. Still she knew she wouldn't be able to avoid having a talk with her mom forever so she had resolved to have the conversation the next day. That way she could leave the following day and not give her mom a lot of time for rebuttal.

"So nice to just be us," her mom had said that morning over coffee. "I love having all you kids home and the grandkids, but it's also nice to just be the two of us, like it used to be. I miss that time."

"I know, mom," and well she did because her mom reminded her every time she was home. Sara had been a surprise. Fourteen years after their daughter Joy had been born, along came Sara. Her mom had thought she was entering menopause when she missed her period, only to experience the tell-tale signs that she was pregnant shortly afterwards, morning sickness, that strange taste in her mouth, her sudden loss of her coffee craving. It had all brought back memories from her past three pregnancies.

She had laughed at the possibility, assuming she must have made a mistake, until the pregnancy test came back positive. Then she had shared a laugh with her husband so that they decided to call her Sara, after Sarah in the Bible who had laughed when she conceived Isaac in her old age.

It had been different this time around. She felt so much less stress, was confident about her ability to parent, although she lacked the energy she had had in her twenties. Sara had truly been a gift to her as she aged. She found she had more time to delight in her little girl than she had with Sara's brothers and sister.

Sara, for her part, took the center stage in the life of her family with daring. She accepted the accolades of her older brothers and sister as her rightful due, relishing their ohs and ahs over her youthful art work and thus forming her desire to be an artist.

Joy had been perturbed at first by the news her mom was pregnant. She had grown comfortable in her favored role as the youngest and only daughter.

"Mom always liked you best."

"Yeah, you were dad's little princess," her brothers, Michael and David, often teased her. Now she had to share that attention. Joy didn't know whether she liked that. Besides, if her mom were pregnant, that meant she and her dad . . . Joy shuddered at the thought.

"That means they actually, you know, did it," she had self-consciously told her best friend, Dale.

Dale had laughed, "They aren't dead you know. I certainly hope they did it."

"Yeah, but they're old. I have to get this mental image out of my mind. As far as I'm concerned, they only did it three times, once for me and my brothers, and now this fourth time."

"You think what you want to think. Anyway, I think it's great."

"You do?"

"Yes, with your mom preoccupied with a new baby, she won't be so focused on you. You'll be able to do more with less interference from home."

"Think again, you don't know my mother," Joy said knowing that would never happen. No matter how much her mom would be busy with the baby, there was no escaping her eagle eye. Besides, between school and her dance classes, how could she find time to do anything more than she was already doing? She had no time to get into trouble. The addition of a new brother or sister wasn't going to change that.

Joy loved to dance. She remembered finally getting her coveted toe shoes after nine years of lessons. She couldn't wait to try them on. They hurt her feet, left her toes bloody, but, oh, the joy of the dance, of seeing what her body could do, pushing herself to her limit and then going further. It was every bit as daunting and consuming as playing football or basketball or running cross country or track. It consumed her life, was her passion. Dale hadn't always understood what it meant to her, often complained about it taking too much of her time, until she pointed out all the time he spent running, cross country in the fall, track in the spring and training during the in-between time.

"I do like running, but it's not an obsession for me, not like you and dancing." Still he had been supportive of her efforts, as she was supportive of him. It had only been in their senior year that he realized he wanted more than friendship.

Joy's dream was to dance with the Ballet Magnificat, a Christian dance group. She had wanted to dance since she had seen her first Nutcracker Ballet production at five. That dream took on flesh once she had seen the Ballet Magnificat when she was six. She loved to dance, lived to dance, and she loved to dance for God, to give God the glory with her whole being. There seemed no worthier goal in life for her. Dale had been supportive of her in this goal as well, even though it meant years apart.

Dale had always been there for her, and she for him, through both of their first crushes and first boyfriend and girlfriend. Dale's dates had resented Dale's friendship with Joy, despite Joy's insistence that they were just friends. On his part, her dates never paid much attention to Dale, perhaps because they had such confidence in their physical prowess and looks. She tended to fall for the star football players but the relationships never lasted long once they realized she would not "put-out" for them. Dale had been different. She had never thought of him that way until he started dating Diane. For some reason Diane had been different from the other girls Dale had dated. The other ones had never been right for Dale, as she had told him. Diane though was different. She was a good fit for Dale. Suddenly Joy felt threatened.

"Is something wrong?" he had asked. "Don't you like Diane?"

"No, she's great, just great. You make a great couple."

"Then what's wrong?"

"I feel like I'm losing my best friend."

"We'll always be friends, Joy."

"No, we won't be able to be friends if you and Diane get serious. Not best friends, the way we have been."

"Joy, if you want me to break up with Diane, I will, but you have to give me more."

"What do you mean?"

"Joy, it's always been you. You're the one for me. I've just been waiting for you, to see if you felt the same way."

"Dale, what are you saying?"

"I'm saying, would you like to go out with me?" Dale waited for Joy to take this in.

"But what about our friendship?" Joy said after a few minutes.

"We'll be even better friends, what better than dating my best friend?"

Joy paused again to think about it.

"Don't think too hard," Dale said and planted a kiss on her lips. Joy pulled back.

"I still want to dance. I'm still planning on joining the Ballet Magnificat after graduation."

"We can work that out. What do you say? I'm not asking for a commitment, just a date."

She paused and smiled, "Yes."

And they'd been dating ever since. While she was busy touring with Ballet Magnificat, Dale became a licensed plumber. Then after years working with other plumbers, learning the ropes of the business, he had started his own business so that when Joy was ready to quit touring he already had his business established.

"But what will I do? I can't give up dancing entirely."

"Why don't you start your own dance studio? I can help with the start-up costs and the business aspects. You just have to recruit students and teach. What do you think?"

Much as she loved dancing, she was feeling the burden on her body. Maybe it was time to move into a new phase of her life, she thought. She had been offered a position with Ballet Magnificat as an instructor but she was ready to return to her roots and her high school sweetheart, so she quit her position and returned to her parents' home, but not for long as she married Dale a year later, setting-up house while establishing her school of dance.

By this time Sara was in middle school. If she had been a precocious child when Joy had left, she was an even more precocious and determined pre-teen as she progressed. Joy was happy to be around to watch her sister's progress in the world and help her mother with this spontaneous burgeoning young woman.

Sara, for her part, was happy to have her big sister around. She was more like a second mother than a sister because of the age difference, still a younger version than the one she had. Sara could talk to Joy about things she couldn't share with her mother.

Still there were good times with her mother, times spent cuddling in front of the TV when school was cancelled because of a blizzard, sipping hot cocoa, laughing and talking. Then as she got older, they would spend mornings sipping coffee together at the kitchen table and go on shopping trips, eating lunch in the food court before going on to another mall in search of bargains. Those had been good times.

"So, how are you doing?" her mother asked.

"I'm fine. I wish everyone would stop asking me that."

"Hey, this is me, mom, no one else around. You can tell me."

"Okay, I'm not okay, but I will be okay if everyone would leave me alone."

"Oh, honey, you don't really want that, to be left alone."

"Yes, I do, at least I think I do."

"What kind of life would that be? You don't want to end up all alone either, that's why this hurts so much. But you won't be alone, a pretty girl like you. You'll find someone else. So what happened, was there another woman?"

"No, mom, not that at all."

"Then what? He seemed like such a nice young man despite being Catholic. What happened? Are you sure there wasn't someone else?" Sara debated how much to tell her mom. Finally she gave in because of her mom's prodding.

"No, there wasn't another woman."

"Then maybe it's just a misunderstanding. You can work it out."

"No, mom, we can't work it out. There wasn't another woman, but there was another man."

"What? What do you mean by that? You didn't cheat on him, did you?"

"No, it's not like that. There was another man because Jeff's gay."

28

Her mother paused in shock before saying, "No, that can't be. He was such a nice young man, he can't be . . . one of those."

"Gay, mom, say the word. It's okay. It's not swearing."

"I, just ... I ... he stayed in our home, ate with us."

"It's not a disease you can catch, mom."

"He played with the grandchildren."

"Mom, he isn't a monster. He's just gay."

"It's an abomination."

"No, it's not."

"Yes, Scripture says so."

"Then Scripture is wrong."

Mary stood up. "Sara, how can you say that?" she said then shook her head, turned aside and continued, talking to herself as much as to her daughter. "It's all because of that awful university. I knew you should have gone to an evangelical college like we wanted you to. Then there would have been none of this, no gay boy-friend, no blasphemy."

"Look, mom, maybe it's not that Scripture is wrong but that our interpretation of Scripture is wrong." Sara continued sitting as her mom paced about the room.

"Oh, no, that's heresy. There is one Scripture, one interpretation."

"Mom, even my friends who attend the evangelical college don't believe that. Anyone who has studied Scripture knows there is room for interpretation."

"I won't listen to this. I'll not have it in my home. And as for your gay boyfriend, I don't want to discuss it any more. We won't talk about such things. And we won't tell your dad, okay?" Mary turned her back on Sara and started banging dishes in the sink.

"Sure, mom, whatever you say," Sara agreed, glad to have the conversation over even if it wasn't how she had wanted it to end.

She went over to Joy's home that afternoon, happy to get away from her mother and the unspoken words.

Once the youngest was down for his nap and the oldest occupied by a video, she had time to talk to Joy one-on-one, just like they used to when Sara was in middle-school and Joy was still living at home. She thought Joy would be more understanding than her mom and she was right.

"Gay? That's too bad, Sara. How are you handling it?"

"I don't know. It feels so strange. I keep wondering, how did I not know? There must have been signs. Why didn't I see them? I feel so stupid."

"But if he didn't even know himself, hadn't come to terms with it . . . Chances are he was pretty good at hiding it, from himself and others. Some gay men are married, living heterosexual lives on the outside, while secretly gay, living double lives of deception."

"But what about their wives? How could they not know?"

"Just because they are gay doesn't mean they can't perform with a woman. Maybe they were able to get away with it. Besides, different people have different levels of sexual desire. Some have sex daily while others are content with once a month, or even less frequently. There are sex-less marriages. I don't know the numbers, I just know they exist, and sometimes they are quite content. Marriage is more than sex." Joy got up and poured herself some more tea.

"I think you dodged a bullet. So much better to know now than to find out after ten years of marriage," she added.

"I guess. I wouldn't want a sex-less marriage. How did you learn so much about this?"

"Sara, I'm a dancer. I'm not saying that every male dancer is gay, still enough of them are," she stated as she sat back down.

"Mom freaked out when I told her."

"Why did you tell her?"

"I had to. She kept prodding and prodding, she wouldn't leave it alone, asking me about Jeff and whether we might get back together again. Now at least she won't ask me that again. She won't even mention Jeff's name." They both laughed.

"So, enough about me. How are you and my newest yet-to-be niece or nephew doing?" Their conversation shifted to Joy's life until disrupted by waking children.

Chapter 8

Sara felt better after talking to Joy, so much so that she was able to get through dinner at home with her parents with a minimum of discomfort despite a little awkwardness. Still, she was ready to head back to her apartment. Let the self-pity begin, she had told herself with a laugh as she faced New Year's alone. She was surprised when Anne came back early as well.

"I thought you weren't coming back until after the New Year," Sara had commented.

"I did too, but after a week at home I remembered why I'm always so happy to get away. It's nice to visit and nice to leave. Besides I heard about a good party. I'm going and so are you."

"But I have plans," Sara protested.

"Unless your plans include a date with a great guy, you're going with me."

"No, but it was a date with a great movie and I've got a bottle of wine with my name on it."

"You can save the movie and wine for another time. If this party is lame, we'll leave early and both enjoy your wine. Deal?"

"Deal."

"Now get out of those sweatpants and into some tight jeans."

Sara was glad for the company. She had had enough time to herself that week, enough time to brood over how her relationship had ended.

"What you need is to get back on the horse, find someone else to date," Anne kept saying whenever she caught her brooding.

"Anne, did you know Jeff was gay before he told me?" Sara asked on the way to the party.

Anne took a deep breathe, paused and looked at Sara before commenting. "I suspected it, yes, but I didn't know."

"Why didn't you say something?"

"What could I have said, Sara, I think your fiancé is a fairy? That would have been well received."

"I guess not. I wouldn't have listened."

"Besides, I didn't know. How could I say something when I wasn't sure?"

"What made you wonder?"

"I'm not sure. Little things, hard to say. Maybe because he wasn't pressuring you to sleep with him, I guess. That always raises questions."

"I thought he was just being a good Christian – that he wanted to wait until we were married because of his beliefs, not because he wasn't interested." They started walking again. "How could I be so naïve," Sara sighed. "Do you think there is something about me that I just can't find the right guy? That I fell for a gay man?" The question had been plaguing Sara for months, ever since she had found out Jeff was gay. Was something wrong with her, she kept asking herself. If she were engaged to a gay man, what did that say about her?

"Sara, don't beat yourself up over this."

"I mean do I give off some radar that scares men away?"

"Don't be ridiculous. Jeff had been attentive, supportive and very affectionate."

"You make him sound like a lap dog," Sara joked.

Anne laughed, "See, now who couldn't like someone with your sense of humor. If I had a mirror I would hold it up in front of you and show you just how great you are."

"Do you think I'm afraid of a 'real' man? Maybe I should just give my virginity away, get it over with. Who am I saving myself for? I may be the only virgin on campus."

"Don't talk nonsense. Sex is not something you just 'give away' to get it over with. You're right to want to save it for the right person. I wish I had."

"But you and Brian were a great couple."

"Were is the operative word, now it's over. Still I'm not beating myself up over it. It didn't work out. I can never go back, just forward."

"At least you know the parts work," Sara said while Anne laughed.

"Sara, trust me, the parts will work when it's the right time and the right person. We have got to find you someone else, and me too," she said as they approached the house with music blaring out of the rafters. "Look out guys, here we come!"

Sara woke up the next day a little hung-over but at least she had refrained from doing anything else she might regret. They had met some men at the party. Brian showed up with some of his friends. It was obvious he had been hoping Anne would be there. Sara wasn't exactly sure what had caused the break-up just before Thanksgiving. She thought it had something to do with family expectations for the holidays, either not wanting her to meet his family or wanting her to meet his family and Anne resisting. Anne hadn't wanted to talk about it and Sara had been so wrapped up in her own problems, she hadn't pursued it. It had been two weeks before she even realized Brian wasn't around anymore.

"Where's Brian?"

"We broke up," Anne stated nonchalantly.

"What? When?"

"Before Thanksgiving. It's no big deal."

"Why didn't you tell me?"

"Nothing to tell. It's over. I don't want to talk about it." And so they hadn't. Brian and Anne weren't back together but they had talked most of the night at the party. Brian had introduced her to his friends. She talked to them for a while but they were clearly not interested. They escaped to get a beer, leaving Sara feeling pathetic and awkward, alone at the party where she didn't know anyone.

"Sara, right?" Sara turned at her name. A man she vaguely remembered from one of her computer classes handed her a beer. "Here, you look thirsty."

"I do, and what does thirsty look like?"

"Like you."

"Do I know you?"

"Sure, we took computer design together last year. I remember you. You sat next to the window and sketched designs while gazing outside instead of paying attention."

"Yeah, that sounds like me." Sara didn't know what else to say. She looked at his face and all she could think of was Jeff. He was shorter than Jeff but at least he was here and appeared to be interested which was more than she could say about Jeff. She accepted the beer and filled the awkward silence with drinking.

"Lame party," he commented. "By the way, I'm Larry."

"Hi, Larry, I'm . . ."

"Sara."

"That's right. You already know my name. What is your major?"

"IT – computer technology."

"You're a good person to know. I'm always running into problems with my computer."

"Then you've got the right person. Here, let me give you my phone number. Next time you have a problem, give me a call," he said as he wrote his number on her hand. Sara was relieved when he excused himself. She decided it was time to find Anne and go.

"Hi, Sara." Someone else who knew her name, Sara thought. She turned around and saw Craig from the basement apartment.

"Hi, Craig."

"I heard you and Jeff broke up. Sorry."

"Yeah, well these things happen."

"So how are you doing?" He had been waiting for an opportunity to talk to Sara once he heard she was no longer engaged. They had passed in the hall but it had never seemed like the right time. He had tried to figure out when to run into her in the laundry room but there were washers and dryers on each floor. It would have been too obvious if he had started using the laundry room on her floor. He hadn't planned on coming to this party but was glad he had.

"I'm fine." There was an awkward silence as Craig tried to come up with something to engage her attention. Just then she saw Jeff come inside heading for the keg. Craig nodded his head in Jeff's direction to alert Sara to his presence.

Sara gasped as she saw Jeff. Too late. He had seen her and saw that she had seen him. There was no easy escape route. She looked at Craig and grabbed his arm, clinging to him and laughing. She didn't want Jeff to think she didn't have a date for New Year's Eve.

"Hi," Jeff said, "how are you?"

"Great, just great," Sara responded, still clinging to Craig's arm, using it to keep her steady. "How are you?"

"Oh, I'm good," a man Sara didn't recognize called Jeff away. "I've got to go. It was good to see you. You look really good," Jeff said as he was led away.

"Awkward," Sara said, letting go of Craig's arm, her face no longer laughing.

"I kind of liked it," Craig said. "That guy's a jerk. He was a fool to let someone like you get away."

"You think so," Sara said, moving away from Craig lest he get the wrong idea.

"Sure. I've seen you coming and going for some time now. You are too good for him."

Sara was relieved to see Anne coming her way. This was her escape route.

"Ready to go?" Anne asked.

"You bet. See you around, Craig," Sara said as they headed for the door.

"So sorry, Sara," Anne said as they walked home. "I didn't think Jeff would be at the party or I wouldn't have insisted on you coming."

"That's okay. I can't avoid him forever, can I? Did you know Brian was going to be there?"

"I didn't know but I had hoped so," Anne responded.

"So . . ." Sara tried to get her to say more.

"So . . . nothing. We talked, nothing else."

Sara was surprised the next afternoon when Craig knocked on her door.

"Hi, Sara, Happy New Year. We didn't get to talk much last night so I thought I would stop by today." He handed her a bouquet of flowers he had managed to get at the mini-mart connected to the gas station. It wasn't much but with so few stores open he figured it was the best he could do. "Mind if I come in?" he asked.

Sara looked back at the apartment, still in disarray from their late night movie watching. "Now isn't a good time," she said.

"Maybe another time?"

"Sure," she said, "That would be nice."

"I'll look forward to it. You know how to reach me," he said as she closed the door. It hadn't been exactly what he had hoped would happen but at least he had his foot in the door. He had waited this long for Sara to come around and could wait longer.

"Who was that?" Anne asked as she came out of the bathroom, towel drying her hair.

"Craig from downstairs. He brought me flowers."

"The guy from the basement, I guess you could do worse."

"I'm not interested. It's still too soon. I'm not ready to start dating again."

"Honey, if you wait until you are ready you'll be a forty-year-old virgin. What will it hurt to go out on one date, see where it takes you?" Sara didn't respond. Yes, what would it hurt, she asked herself.

Chapter 9

"Joy Reese," Joy heard her name as if in a fog, from some distant place. She had been lost in thought while awaiting her appointment. She put the magazine she had failed to read back with the others and followed the arrows down the hall to the next waiting room on her journey.

She felt the small flutter of new life inside her, assuring her that the changes to her body were no illusion. Pregnant with her third child, it still wasn't routine. Every pregnancy was different. Her first two pregnancies had been very different. In comparison to her daughter's emergence into life, her pregnancy for her son had been a breeze, some morning sickness, some distaste in her mouth, but nothing like with her daughter. Then she had been miserable for three months. The symptoms had abated some in her second trimester, but still, her whole body had reacted to this little invader and during the last few months she could hardly sleep as the baby had somersaulted in her stomach all night, dancing to a music only she heard.

In contrast, her son had been so much easier. She had been grateful for that. Another pregnancy like the first and it would have been the last. She had so wanted a large family that she had been brave enough to try again, hoping this pregnancy would be easier, and it was. It was a good thing too for her daughter who had been demanding in utero, was equally demanding on the outside, mixing up her days with her nights, keeping her awake with colic. This little girl was definitely her own being from birth, from the moment of conception. If something so small could have a personality, she did.

She knew from the start with her first two pregnancies. As a dancer she was trained to listen to her body, be in tune to subtle changes others might miss, while also ignoring them when necessary to perform. It was a strange balance of neglect and care, her life in ballet. Now that she was teaching, it was a little easier. Not so much pressure to perform, to be perfect. Still she felt an inner pressure to perfection that wasn't the same as hearing her old dance instructor scold her for day-dreaming and losing focus. It was worse because she was her own worst critic. But then, trying to dance, to go on pointe while pregnant had been a whole new challenge. How could she keep balance and be graceful when waddling like a duck. At least that was how she felt, like she was waddling during those last months.

She tried to maintain a healthy weight throughout her pregnancies. She tried to remain active. Her doctor had assured her that the more active she remained, the better for her and for her baby. So she had continued to teach dance at her studio while carrying a new life within and then while caring for her baby daughter. Ashley was three when her brother, Jacob, came along. Joy had hoped having a baby brother might inspire Ashley to be more careful, to be helpful. She had read that it was best to have a girl first because the girl would then help with subsequent babies. Who was she kidding anyway? Who were these experts? They definitely had not known Ashley. Still, Joy had seen some glimmer of big sisterly care for the precious new baby.

With Ashley in kindergarten and Jacob almost potty-trained it had seemed like a good time for another baby. She was excited to meet this new gift from God, wondered how this pregnancy would be different from the first two. So far it had been relatively easy; did that mean it would be a boy? Joy resisted the urge to decide which it was. She didn't want to know ahead of time, she wanted to be surprised at birth.

Each pregnancy had been its own gift to her. Dale and she had been praying for a baby. Then one day she felt this experience of oneness with God, a sense of co-creation that she couldn't quite understand or put into words. When she missed her next period and found out she was pregnant she remembered this encounter with God while in prayer and felt God had been present from the very moment of conception. Two years later when she felt the same experience while in prayer she thought it was just a beautiful reminder from God about that other time, only to find out weeks later she was pregnant.

She had had no such experience with this pregnancy. Maybe she had been too busy chasing after two preschoolers to listen as intently to her body as she had back then. Still she had no doubt that God had been just as present in this pregnancy as the other times. Her stomach rounded quicker with this pregnancy, stretched out from the previous two. And she wondered what new blessing awaited her from this child.

The life of a young mother was full of many challenges, was exhausting as she found she needed her afternoon naps long after her children were ready to give up theirs. Still, in those moments when they were asleep or quietly engrossed in play, she realized she was blessed. She tried to relish each moment, knowing that time passed more quickly than she could imagine. Already she had sent one off to school. Before she knew it her daughter would be grown-up and leaving her with her son not far behind. She needed to relish this time, despite how tired she was at times, despite being pulled apart by so many demands.

Dale had been supportive, which made a huge difference. He was involved in their children's lives, truly being a co-parent, giving her a break when she needed one, working out his schedule to fit both of their jobs. Fortunately her babies had been welcome additions at her school of dance. There were always mothers of older children around, waiting to hold a baby when she was occupied with classes and Dale wasn't able to be home. Her teenage assistants were also great helpers. Ashley and Jacob both loved spending time at the dance school, loved all the other children, the commotion and the attention they received. They were often reluctant to leave when Dale came to pick them up. And once they were old enough to be included in pre-school classes, Joy signed them up.

As the owner of his own business, Dale worked long hours but had a flexible schedule and so was able to adjust to a certain extent in order to work around her timetable, sick kids and doctor appointments. He was due home at noon today so she could keep her appointment this afternoon for a follow-up to her most recent mammogram. It was nothing she was concerned about. She knew the routine, had been through it before. She had "lumpy" breasts, fibrocystic they had called it - multiple cysts in her breasts. When her doctor had first noticed the lumps and sent her for her first mammogram, she had been worried. When a repeat had been scheduled, followed by an ultrasound, she had been more worried. That had been over five years ago, before Ashley had been born. Now it was old hat to her. Because of the lumps, her doctor had her getting mammograms once a year as a precaution. Joy didn't like the idea, wondering about all the excess radiation from the yearly mamms at such an early age, but had reluctantly agreed to go along with the doctor, pushed by Dale.

"There's no sense in taking unnecessary chances," Dale had said.

So, at thirty-four, she was already used to the routine of mamms and follow-ups any time a cyst looked a little different. It was a pain, one she had considered skipping this year, especially because of her pregnancy, but Dale had insisted so she had relented.

"How many times do I have to go through this?" she muttered to herself, "Unnecessary radiation, a waste of time." Joy had already discussed this with her doctor who was well aware of her resistance to this course of treatment. She made her second trip to the hospital to the radiation department and was sitting in the waiting area, her top covered by a hospital gown while she waited for the all clear so she could get dressed and go home.

She was escorted back into the radiologist's office.

"Now this is new," she thought but continued confident it was nothing.

"A couple of the cysts have grown significantly since last year and look suspicious. We would like to schedule a biopsy of the lumps at your earliest convenience as a precaution."

"It's just a precaution?" Joy asked.

"Yes, there is an indeterminate mass in your right breast that we want to check out. I'll send the results to your doctor so you can set up a time for the biopsy."

"I'm pregnant."

"Yes, I saw that on your chart. This will be a simple procedure, local anesthetic. It won't hurt your baby and will give you peace of mind."

"Okay, sure, let's get this over with," Joy said.

"You can finish getting dressed and we'll see about scheduling that biopsy."

Joy wondered just who he meant by this royal "we." Maybe he thought it made him sound more authoritative, using the plural to indicate it's not just his opinion. She would see about this, she told herself. She set up the appointment but would talk it over with Dale before going through with it. She ruminated the whole drive home.

"What a waste of my time. Another wild goose chase to find nothing. So what, I have lumpy breasts?" she thought to herself, determined she would not keep the appointment

"Of course you're keeping the appointment," Dale said when she told him.

"But . . ."

"No buts about it. If there's any chance that there is a problem, we will deal with it right now, not wait till it gets worse." He couldn't bring himself to say the big C.

"It's nothing. I know my body and I'm sure I would know if there was something wrong. They'll put me through a battery of tests and cut into me all for nothing. Wasted time and wasted money. I wonder how much this will cost us. You know we've got to be careful about every penny, what with the new baby."

"I won't hear you making medical decisions based on money. We'll get by. Have I ever not been able to provide for you and the kids?"

"No, I guess not."

"We'll get by, besides, it won't be for nothing. Aren't you worried? I know I am."

"Yes, a little, but if I let myself get worried every time something suspicious shows up on my mamms, what kind of life would that be?"

"Then don't worry, but do this for me."

Dale had managed to take the time off from work and they had arranged for a baby sitter so he could be with her for the biopsy.

"We won't get a result right away. They have to send it away," Joy had protested. "My mom could go with me."

"That's okay. I want to be with you."

"Okay," Joy agreed. Despite her protestations, she was worried; she just wasn't letting herself think about it.

She was glad for his presence as she waited her turn for the procedure. How many others were enduring the same process, facing the same possibility, she asked herself. Certainly she was not alone, yet she was feeling alone even as she patted the growing life within her. "I'm not alone," she reassured herself as she reached for her husband's hand.

She sat in her doctor's office later that week. Again Dale had arranged to be with her. In the past she had gotten results over the phone. Of course in the past she hadn't had a biopsy. Still she felt that the need to come in person to get results from her doctor was not a harbinger of good tidings.

"More time off work, there better be a problem or I'll be pretty angry," she had joked with Dale on the way there.

Dale had attempted to smile, then reaching over, taking one hand off of the steering wheel, he had squeezed her hand.

They were seated in the doctor's office, waiting for her to get away from the exam rooms to talk to them. She walked in, shook both of their hands with a warm, yet concerned expression on her face. She proceeded to sit down and opened Joy's file which had been placed on her desk. After looking over the report she looked up.

"I'm afraid your recent biopsy came back positive for cancer, in fact it appears to be invasive lobular cancer, ILC. That's why your mamm didn't catch it."

"Invasive . . ." Joy started.

"Lobular Cancer, ILC for short. It doesn't always form in lumps but rather as tentacles that spread out, making it harder to diagnose. I want to refer you to a specialist to make sure you get the best possible care."

"What about our baby?" Joy asked.

"The cancer specialist will know better what your options are. Fortunately you are not too far into the second trimester so an abortion may be safely performed with little harm to you if necessary."

"No, no abortion. No one is going to hurt my baby."

"I didn't say it was necessary, just that it was an option."

"Not for me," Joy insisted.

"Well, why don't you talk that over with the oncologist? No decision needs to be made today," her doctor said. "I'm recommending that you see Dr. Russell. I've worked with him before. He's one of the best. He'll be able to explain your options to you."

"Abortion is not an option," Joy continued to insist.

"You can discuss that with him. I'll have the receptionist set up an appointment, but in light of the results, I want you to get in to see him as soon as possible." She wrote out Dr. Russell's contact info on a card and gave it to Dale.

"Any questions?" she asked him.

"No, I guess not, not till we talk to Dr. Russell," he said.

"Again, I'm sorry about this. I will be in touch with Dr. Russell. I will work closely with him on this, especially in regards to your pregnancy and other health issues," she said as she stood up, indicating their time was over.

"Thank you," Dale said as he gently guided Joy to a standing position and led her out the door.

"No one is going to hurt my baby," Joy continued to insist as they drove home.

Once the kids were down for the night, she got on the internet and did a web search: breast cancer and pregnancy. At first she was discouraged. The first few sites told her little more than she already knew. Radiation was out during pregnancy, some chemos were considered safe, but further down the list she found what she had been looking for, not just more up-to-date treatment options but stories of others who had experienced the same condition.

"What are you doing?" Dale asked, surprised to find her still up.

"Researching breast cancer and pregnancy."

He leaned over to look at the computer screen. "And what have you found?"

"That we are not alone," she said. "While not common, it's becoming more common as more women are waiting longer to have children, and there are options, more options than just terminating the pregnancy or delaying treatment till after birth."

He hugged her as they gazed at the screen together. "You coming to bed?" he asked.

"Not just yet. Go ahead. I won't be long," she assured him, giving him a kiss.

When they went to their next appointment she came armed with all of her new found knowledge.

Chapter 10

The meeting with Dr. Russell had not been encouraging. He had wanted to begin aggressive treatment, chemo therapy to shrink the tumor, then if the chemo is successful a lumpectomy followed by radiation, which would have proven deadly to the baby. Joy turned down anything that would harm the small life growing within her.

"This is a particularly aggressive form of cancer. If we don't treat it, it could grow faster than your baby. We could end up losing both of you."

"No," Joy had insisted. "What can I do without hurting my baby?"

"Some types of chemo will not harm your baby. We can hold off on treatment, but there is no guarantee we'll be able to save your life if we don't act now."

"I'd rather take that chance than lose my baby. Besides, I've read that you can safely treat breast cancer while pregnant."

"You're correct. There are more options now than before. The latest research indicates that certain chemotherapies are safe to use during pregnancy. The chemicals don't pass through the placenta to the baby. Surgery is also considered safe, though depending on the surgery we usually recommend radiation which is not safe to a growing fetus."

"What do you recommend?" Dale asked.

"I would terminate the pregnancy, do chemo followed by surgery and radiation – but it's not my choice. It's up to you. Because of the aggressive nature of this form of cancer I would not recommend that we wait to begin treatment. We could do chemo and see if it shrinks the tumor so we can do a lumpectomy."

"And if that doesn't work?" Dale asked.

"We would do a mastectomy, possibly a double mastectomy, then seven weeks of radiation, but that's only if the chemo doesn't work. With any luck the chemo will work so a mastectomy won't be required. We typically like to stop chemo the month before delivery to avoid the chance of infection because of a weakened immune system. If all goes well we could do the lumpectomy before the baby is born. We would still follow up with radiation but that won't be necessary until after the baby is born."

"Will I be able to breast feed my baby?"

"Not while receiving chemo but we should be done with that before the baby is born. If you chose to have a mastectomy after giving birth you will not be able to breast feed because we would want the breasts to shrink back to normal before surgery."

"Will it just be my right breast or both?"

"Let's wait till we get the results from the latest test about the possibility of recurrence. There is no history of breast cancer in your family so that is a positive factor, however you do have a number of lumps and this particular cancer can be tricky. All points to consider."

"If I have the lumpectomy, does that mean I won't require additional surgery?"

"There's no guarantee."

"What do you suggest?" Dale asked again.

"We don't have to decide today but we shouldn't wait too long. We can wait for the additional test results. We still don't have the results on the Oncotype DX score which will give you the probability of recurrence based on your genes. The results should be back in a week. In the mean time you can take some time to talk it over, think about your options, before deciding," Dr. Russell said.

Joy hadn't wanted to go along with this. Her mind was made up, but Dale had silenced her with a look and stood up.

"Thank you, Doctor. We'll talk it over and get back to you," he said as he shook Dr. Russell's hand.

"You can't possibly be thinking about killing our baby," Joy stormed at him the minute they were alone in their car.

"Joy, you heard what he said. We may lose both of you. Our kids need their mother. I need you. We can have other children once this is taken care of. I can't just let you go without a fight."

"We don't know that. We don't know that I won't make it. Dale, how can I let anyone harm this life I have growing within me? How can I let them take my baby, our baby? It's certain death for our baby if we do this, not certain death for me. I'm willing to take the chance."

"But I don't know that I'm willing to take a chance on losing you. We can have other children."

"But it won't be this baby, this child. We'll never know this child. I will always regret it."

"Will you at least think about it? Give it some thought. We can discuss it later. Maybe we can talk it over with our pastor."

Joy agreed with this but she knew. Her mind was made up; there would be no bending to his will in this. Now how to get him to accept this?

Chapter 11

"Something wrong?" his roommate asked him. Jeff hadn't been his usual self for the past week, not since New Year's Eve. He wondered, had something happened then? He hadn't been going to ask, usually stayed out of Jeff's business, especially since he had broken up with Sara. But what was up with that, he wondered.

They were roommates out of convenience, nothing more. For the most part they didn't do anything together or talk much except for the normal roommate discussions about rent, bills, and bringing home a girl. Andrew had met Sara and liked her but didn't know much about her other than that she and Jeff were engaged and she was an art major. He was fine with that. He was also fine when Jeff didn't take advantage of the roommate code in regards to overnight dates. It made life easier for him and his dates.

Jeff had been very obliging about the women he had over. Having two bedrooms made life so much easier than when they had been in the dorm. He would never have been able to afford an apartment on his own, so splitting the rent with Jeff had been a god-send. He was about as close to an ideal roommate as one could get. But then he broke up with Sara and he started staying out till all hours of the night, sometimes not coming home at all, not like him at all. Andrew didn't worry too much about it as long as Jeff came through with his share of the rent and other expenses. Still it was curious. Jeff was not acting like himself at all. Since New Year's all of that had stopped abruptly and now here he was, staying in the apartment, brooding.

"Nothing's wrong," Jeff said with no conviction in his voice. "Why do you ask? Do I look like something is wrong?"

"Well, yes, you do. You are just not your usual happy-go-lucky self. Even after you broke up with Sara, you didn't brood or mope around the apartment like you have the past few weeks."

"I'm sorry if I'm underfoot or have inconvenienced you by staying in my apartment."

"No inconvenience. I was just wondering." Their roommate agreement had been based on their not getting involved in each other's life. He realized he had broken the agreement by saying something, still he wasn't entirely unfeeling. "Sorry I said anything."

"No, that's okay. I'm sorry I snapped at you." Andrew wondered if this was an opening to say more, looked at Jeff and decided to keep his mouth shut. Why mess up a perfectly good roommate situation with unnecessary questions?

"Hey, I'm going to have some friends over to watch the game on Sunday, in case you want to join us." This was his peace offering.

"No, thanks, I need to work on a research paper, but thanks for letting me know. I'll plan on going to the library that day."

"If you change your mind, you're welcome. You know, beer, pizza, chips, football. What better way to spend a Sunday afternoon?" Jeff could think of some better ways but not much better.

It felt like he had been on a roller coaster the past two months, or maybe more like the Demon Drop. He just kept going up. Eventually he knew he would have to crash, and crash he did. He had gone a little crazy with his new found discovery about himself. There was an active gay scene in the area and he jumped into it. Gay bars, illicit rendezvous, partying till all hours of the night. He had experimented with his new life style, having finally accepted who he was. He wanted to try it all, make up for lost time, but after two months he was starting to realize that this wasn't who he was either. His new promiscuous life-style after living much like a monk for several years didn't fit him either. It had all hit him when he saw Sara at the New Year's Eve party.

"So that's Sara," his latest date had asked. "Who's that guy she's hanging on? Seems she's gotten over you."

"Just a creep who lives in her apartment building. Sara can do better than him." He felt a twinge of something. He wasn't sure what. Not jealousy. He knew that part of his life was over, but something else. Guilt? Sadness over any pain he may have caused her, sadness over what he had lost, even though he had known he could no longer live a lie. If only he had realized sooner, maybe they could have been friends. He wouldn't have hurt Sara for anything and yet he had. And what was she doing with that jerk, Craig? She must be feeling pretty low to result to a relationship with him. Still it was none of his business, hadn't been his business since they had broken up. He just wanted her to be happy, and wanted to be happy himself, but he didn't know how.

Had he been wrong? He found himself asking the question he had been avoiding for the past two months. If a heterosexual life with Sara had not been right for him, the way he was living now wasn't right either. Neither were true to who he was. Perhaps there was another way. There had to be another way. He just needed to find it. A way between living a lie, hurting another girl by a lie, and living a life of one-night stands. He wasn't sure what this way was but he knew he couldn't continue down his current path. He had withdrawn from all of his new contacts and spent the last few weeks brooding.

There was someone who could help, he thought. Doug, Doug could help. Doug knew him better than he knew himself. He hadn't talked to Doug since Doug had told him he was gay. He didn't know why he hadn't contacted him. Maybe because he had been such a jerk when Doug had told him. More guilt. No wonder he had kept moving for the past months. He had been avoiding all the layers of guilt. No, Doug wasn't the person to talk to, at least not yet. He called Mike.

"Can we talk?"

"Sure, come on over." Mike had been expecting this call, though he had not thought it would take Jeff so long to make it. More thick-headed than many, he thought to himself. He had seen the path Jeff had taken, had seen others take the same path, and had been waiting for Jeff to wake up and realize this wasn't the right way for him.

"Jeff's coming over," he told Chris.

"About time," Chris responded. They were leaders in Dignity. As such they knew there was another way to be gay than the path Jeff had been trying out. They were both active in church. They too had tried the gay scene and found it lacking. Now they were in a committed relationship to each other, one not sanctioned by their church, but sanctioned in their hearts and minds by their God. It had been a hard road to get to this place of acceptance of themselves. It had been hard to find a love that lasted. It had been hard to find a God that accepted not condemned them, but they had. And now that they had, they were helping others find their way to acceptance as well.

Chapter 12

Craig had continued to be attentive. She seemed to run into him every time she left the building and upon her return. It was almost creepy, like he has lying in wait for her. She dismissed that thought, reminding herself how nice it was to feel desirable, especially after the blow her ego had taken. She didn't trust herself where men were concerned. After all, if she had been so mistaken where Jeff was concerned, perhaps she was mistaken about Craig.

"Didn't I see you talking to some other guy at the party?" Anne had questioned her.

"Yeah, a guy from one of my computer classes. He had given me his phone number, wrote it on my hand." She looked down where only a blurred imprint of ink remained. "What was I thinking? I washed it off before writing it down. I guess it wasn't meant to be," Sara chided herself.

"See, two men in one night. And you thought you couldn't find anyone."

"I don't know that I want anyone."

"Sure you do, stop kidding yourself, get . . ."

"Back on the horse and ride," Sara finished Anne's sentence. They both laughed.

She went downstairs, on her way to class. There was Craig again.

"Mind if I walk with you?" he asked. Sara paused momentarily then agreed. She found it easier to talk to Craig while both were walking. Something about moving forward, keeping your eyes straight ahead, having something to do, made it easier to talk than trying to make chit-chat at a party.

"You want to get something to eat later today, my treat?"

"Sure, why not," she found herself agreeing.

Dating Craig took her mind off of Jeff. It did feel good to be wanted, to be deemed desirable. Craig started walking her to classes whenever he had a class in the general area, sometimes even when he did not. It didn't feel as free and easy as her relationship with Jeff, in fact she found herself irritated with Craig at times despite herself and before she knew it they would be fighting. Jeff and she had never fought. Craig seemed a little possessive. One date and it was as if they were "going together" in his eyes. She hadn't wanted that. She just wanted to go out, play the field, feel desirable again. She had thought that Craig would be the answer to that. She had been wrong.

At least he found her desirable. Their second date he was already presuming to go to third base, wherever that was. She hadn't been sure, had never been instructed in the bases. She just knew that good girls kept their pants on. As long as she did that, she figured she would be okay.

He had planted wet kisses all over her face and clumsily groped her breast, entreating her to go into his apartment.

"No," she had said, pushing him away. Craig backed off, biding his time.

"I don't know what is wrong with me," Sara said later to Anne. "Craig's okay. I just don't feel that way about him. Do you think there's something wrong with me?"

"Did you feel 'that' way about Jeff?"

"Of course I did. I liked kissing him, wanted more. Maybe it's still too soon."

"Or maybe Craig isn't the one for you."

"Maybe, maybe I better end it before it goes any further."

"Might be a good idea, if there is no spark, maybe there will never be one."

"A lot of maybe's" Sara commented. Hard to make a decision on maybes, she thought. She decided that she needed to put the brakes on the relationship with Craig, not that they had a "relationship." Two dates and walking to class together don't a relationship make, do they, she questioned. She didn't want to be leading him on or taking advantage of him. But what should she say, she wondered. She could pretend to be busy next time he asked her out, but he lived in the same building as she did. He would know. Dating was difficult, she thought.

They were walking across campus together.

"So, how about a movie this weekend?" Craig asked.

Sara prepared to say no when she saw Jeff heading in their direction. She grabbed Craig's arm, just as she had at the party, before she could think better about it.

"Hi Sara, Craig," he acknowledge Craig then turned to Sara. "Good to see you again."

"Good to see you, too," Sara responded.

"Can I talk to you for a moment?" he asked. Sara looked at Craig, let go of his arm and agreed. "It will just be a minute," she told Craig when he began to protest. Craig stepped back to give them some space.

"Can I see you sometime? There's something I have to talk to you about."

"Sure," Sara agreed, "when?" Her heart thumped. This was what she had been waiting for. He had come to his senses, realized that this whole gay thing had just been a big mistake and wanted her back.

"I can't talk now. I'm on my way to class. Maybe tonight. We could get a pizza." They arranged to meet at their favorite pizza place that night.

"What was that about?" Craig asked.

"I don't know. He said he wants to talk."

"So how about this weekend, a movie?" Craig asked again as they reached the apartment building.

"I don't know. I'll let you know later," because later I might be engaged again, she found herself thinking despite herself.

She was late getting to the pizza place, not wanting to seem too eager.

"I've already ordered," he told her. He had ordered their regular, pineapple, ham and green olives, their version of the Hawaiian.

"How have you been?" Jeff started, "you look good."

"I've been okay, keeping busy."

"So, are you and Craig an item?"

"Not at all. We've been on a couple of dates."

"Good, you can do better."

"What about you? Seeing anyone?"

"Not really. That's not what I wanted to talk to you about," he said.

"So talk." Their pizza arrived, putting an end to conversation as they helped themselves to a few bites.

"Ummm, so good. I haven't had one of these since the last time we were here. Remember last October, before . . ." she stopped abruptly. It had felt so good, so natural to be here with him. She didn't want to bring up the unpleasant circumstances of their break-up.

"That's what I wanted to talk to you about." Here it comes, Sara thought, her stomach rolling at the thought. He wants to get back together.

"I wanted to apologize."

"For what, the break-up?"

"Not the break-up, just for how I did it, the whole thing." This was not where Sara had hoped the conversation would go.

"I'm so sorry, Sara, sorry about the whole relationship."

"I'm not sorry."

"I never should have misled you. I'm sorry because I lied to you, I lied to myself. I had been running away from myself, this side of myself, since I was a kid. Getting engaged to you was another way to run away. I recognize now that not only was that unfair to you, it was unfair to me. I never meant to hurt you."

"So you're not here to get back together?"

"No, no, is that what you thought?"

"No, of course not," she lied, "well, maybe a little," she admitted. "After all, our favorite pizza at our favorite place . . ."

"I'm so sorry if I gave you that impression. It wasn't my intention at all. I keep making a mess of things." Jeff paused before continuing, "I'm gay, that's not going to change, but hopefully I can accept that and not mislead others or myself. I'm not proud of how I acted after our break-up. I went a little crazy. But now I'm back to myself, trying to be me, trying to make amends. I've realized that if I'm ever to be at peace with myself, I need to make amends wherever I hurt others. I know I hurt you. If you could find it in your heart to forgive me, maybe we could be friends. I would really like that."

Sara stared down at her pizza. It no longer tasted terrific; instead it looked like a mass of fat and grease on a piece of cardboard.

"I'm sorry, Jeff. I can't do this right now, not today, maybe not ever. If you want forgiveness maybe you should see your priest." Sara stood up. "Now, I think it's time for me to leave."

"I'm not making excuses, I'm not looking for absolution, I just want to make amends," Jeff stated. "I want us to be friends."

Sara hurried out without responding. She rushed home. She hadn't realized how much she still cared about Jeff, how much she was hanging on to the hope of them getting back together until she had seen him today. Now that hope had been quashed, brought out into the bright light of day where it evaporated. She was crying as she reached her apartment building. There was Craig again. Would he just leave me alone, she thought.

"Sara, you okay?"

"Just leave me alone."

"Was it Jeff? Did he do anything? I ought to cream that fag."

"Don't say that, don't call him that."

"But that's what he is. Don't you know that by now?"

"Just leave me alone. I'm okay. Just let me pass." Craig stepped back and let her climb the stairs.

"Faggot," he said to himself. "I ought to take care of him," he muttered.

"I take it dinner with Jeff didn't go well," Anne said as she walked in.

"No, not at all. I'm an idiot. I really thought he wanted us to get back together again."

"Oh, Sara, I could have told you that wasn't going to happen. Gay is not a coat you can put on or take off."

"I know. I just hoped he was wrong, that he had made a mistake," Sara cried the tears she hadn't allowed herself to cry before.

"It's okay. Go ahead and cry. I know it hurts but maybe now you can finally accept this and get on with your life." Sara doubted that.

Chapter 13

Craig had been afraid he had blown it with Sara last night when he had called Jeff a fag. That was what he was; still Sara didn't like language like that. He tried to watch his language around her, knowing she didn't like any kind of foul language, knowing that she attended church each Sunday. He had come too far to blow it now, he told himself. He had been relieved when she had let him walk her to class again, as if nothing had happened. Neither said anything about the previous night.

"So, you want to go to a movie or something this weekend?"

"Sure," Sara agreed. That was a good sign, he thought. Was it time to make his move?

The movie had been okay, nothing exceptional. Sara had been quiet on the way there and back. He wasn't sure what had happened. She was somehow different. It was as if something had shifted inside her. He didn't know what but he knew it was something. Perhaps this incident with Jeff had been what she had needed to finally let him go, he thought. Either way, she had not pulled away when he put his arm around her during the movie.

He had been surprised when Sara accepted his invitation for coffee in his apartment. It was the first time she had agreed to this despite repeated invitations.

"Just a minute," he said as he went inside, quickly picked up clothes scattered about the small efficiency, sticking them in a closet, piling dishes in the sink to make the room somewhat presentable. Then he opened the door and welcomed Sara inside. She sat down on his futon that doubled as his bed while he got coffee started. Then he joined her.

"You're awfully quiet. Is something wrong?"

"No, nothing," Sara said while he moved closer. She leaned over and kissed him with a force that surprised him.

"What about the coffee?" he asked then quickly shut up, aroused by her passion. They kissed long and hard then planted quick, feverish kisses about their faces and neck. Craig reached in excitement, caressing Sara's breast. He reached further down to her panty line and started to unzip her jeans when Sara suddenly stopped.

"Wait," she said.

"What do you mean, wait?" Craig said, continuing to kiss her and fumble at her jeans. "You know you want it."

"No, I don't, stop," she said pulling away from him.

"Don't worry. I know you're a virgin. I'll be gentle with you," he said, his passion unabated as he pulled her back to him.

"I said no," Sara said, pushing him away and standing up.

Craig wasn't giving up so easily. He stood up, put his hands on either side of her and said, "Okay, we'll go slow. I didn't mean to rush you." He leaned in for another long, slow kiss. "How about that coffee?"

"No, I have to go. I have to get out of here," Sara said as she reached for her coat.

"Now wait a minute. You're the one who kissed me, you started this."

"And now I want to end it. I've changed my mind. It just isn't right."

"What's wrong? You gay like your faggot boyfriend?" Craig felt his anger rise as quickly as his passion as he grabbed Sara.

"And if I were, what's it to you?" she said stomping on the top of his foot and letting herself out. Craig cringed in pain. He limped back to the futon and gently massaged his foot. The smell of fresh brewed coffee began to fill the room.

"That didn't go well," he told himself as he continued to rub his foot.

"What a jerk," Sara told herself as she stormed upstairs. A jerk indeed, she thought but this time she didn't know whether she was referring to Craig or herself. "What a jerk," she repeated to herself.

"What's wrong?" Sara was grateful for Anne's presence. Anne was solid and real amidst the confusion that was her life. "How was your date?"

"I made a pass at Craig."

"Good for you."

"No, not good. It was stupid. It was wrong. I just wanted to prove to myself that I could do this, but then I couldn't go through with it. I just don't feel that way about Craig."

"And what way is that?"

"You know, I'm not in love with him."

"I thought this was about sex. What's love got to do with it?"

Sara knew Anne was teasing her, trying to lighten the situation, but there was also some truth in what she had said. What did love have to do with it? This was about sex, pure and simple, or so she had thought.

"Aren't you attracted to Craig?"

"Yes, no, not really, some. It just wasn't right. I just wanted a meaningless fling to assure me that I'm desirable and all the parts work, but then I couldn't go through with it." Sara sat down on the couch next to Anne. "Maybe there is something wrong with me."

"Sara, there's nothing wrong with you. You just haven't found the right person yet."

"Craig accused me of being gay."

"Cheap shot. That's a pretty sad attempt to get someone to sleep with him. You are better off without him."

"But what if I am gay? Do you think that was why I fell in love with   a   gay   man?

"The operative word here is man. Sara, you just said you had fallen in love with a man, regardless of whether he was gay or not. You are attracted to men, plain and simple. Have you ever found yourself attracted to a woman?"

"No, I guess not, but maybe that's because I never thought of it as an option."

"Let me assure you, if you have never had a crush on a woman, chances are you are not a lesbian. It's not something you just wake up one day and decide after a botched relationship. There would have been signs long before now."

Sara appreciated Anne's support. Anne was so supportive and understanding. Why couldn't men be like that, she wondered. What would it be like to kiss her, she found herself wondering, much to her surprise. "Where had that come from?" she asked herself.

"I guess you are right," she said getting up. "I'm going to bed." She wanted to get out of there to think about what had just happened.

"You sure? We could put in a video?"

"No, I've had a long night. Time to get some sleep," Sara said and got ready for bed. She tossed and turned, going over the events of the night. She didn't know what was going on inside her. Where did those feelings for Anne come from? She brought all of her confusion to God, asking for guidance but getting none.

"At least you have a choice," a voice inside her said. A choice? What did that mean? Where had the voice come from? Of course if she had a choice, she would choose to be heterosexual. Who would choose to be despised if they had a choice? What did the voice mean? Did it mean that others didn't have a choice? Jeff didn't have a choice, not if he were to be true to himself? But why did she have a choice?

So much to think about, she told herself. Thoughts for another day she assured herself as she finally managed to sleep. But what did the voice mean?

Chapter 14

The holidays had come and gone. She managed to make a little extra money from working weekends providing food samples at Sam's Club and was receiving unemployment. Every week she sent out more applications, made follow-up phone calls for potential jobs, but had not as yet found anything permanent. Esther wasn't quite ready to settle for a job at McDonald's or Pizza Hut. She figured as long as she had unemployment she could hold off for a while, while figuring out what to do next. It wasn't a bad situation. It was kind of nice to get paid while she looked for something else. If only she knew what that something else looked like. It would be nice if it included health benefits. She qualified for a subsidy for health benefits, still even with the subsidy, the cost was hard to justify with so little income coming in. But going without at her age and with her health problems was out of the question.

She had been delighted at Dale and Joy's news about the pregnancy. A new baby was always a gift she had told them. They were coming over for dinner tonight. She was using her extra time in "semi-retirement" to have more time with her family, making home-made meals she didn't have time to make when she was working. She benefitted because she got to see her son, daughter-in-law and grandchildren more often. They benefitted because Joy was relieved of the burden of planning a meal. Everyone won.

Dale had said there was something they wanted to talk to her about when she had called to invite them.

"Is everything all right with the baby?" That had been her first concern.

"The baby's fine. See you tonight, mom," he had reassured her.

If the baby was fine, what else could be wrong, she had wondered. As long as the baby was fine, everything else would be okay, she told herself. No sense in borrowing trouble, there was enough real trouble to deal with than imagining the worst. Still, it was so hard when your children are sick or hurting. She remembered it too well from her days with her babies. So frightening and frustrating when babies are sick. They can't tell you what is wrong.

You have to guess and hope you get it right. So much better to be sick yourself than to have sick children, she remembered. Still, taking care of children while being sick was no picnic either. Fortunately her two grandsons were made of sturdy stock. They had the usual number of colds and bugs, but nothing more serious.

Dale reached for Joy's hand and smiled at here as they drove over to his mom's. The kids were poking each other in the back seat.

"Quiet down back there," he said then looked over at Joy. "You up for this?"

"Sure, we've got to tell her sometime, best to get it over with," she said as she thought over the events of the last few weeks.

Joy had appreciated the breathing space the doctor had given them to make their decision. At four months the baby was far enough along to not be in danger if they started chemo. Still Joy thought every week without chemicals was a plus.

"We don't want to put this off too long," Dale had insisted during one of their many discussions. "We want to give the baby the best chance possible but not at the risk of your life." Dale had finally come to her way of thinking in regards to keeping the baby, but he still was concerned about her. Joy's primary concern remained her baby.

"I know, but you heard the doctor, we can wait a while yet."

"I just don't know what I would do if I ever lost you," he told her with a squeeze of her hand.

"I know, I know, I don't want to leave you or the kids either, but we've still got time to consider our options," Joy had reassured him, while inside she was completely lost. She wanted to do what was best for her babies, all three of her babies, but she wasn't as clear on what that was as she appeared to be on the outside.

"God, haven't I dedicated my life to you? Why this? Why now? I don't want to leave my babies. I can't allow anyone to hurt this new life growing inside of me. What do I do?" Joy asked in her prayers and received no answer. One thing she did know was that she believed abortion was wrong. She held on to that belief. She couldn't imagine God ever telling her to kill her own baby so despite her lack of response from God in prayer, she thought she knew what to do.

"God doesn't always speak to us in ways we understand. More often than not, God is silent," her pastor said when they consulted him.

"What do we do then?" Joy asked.

"Look to Scripture, study God's word and use your intellect. God gave it to you for a reason. If you have felt no sense of what God wants, use your brain."

They made a list of pros and cons about terminating her pregnancy. Pros were that the doctor could pursue aggressive treatment without worrying about harming their child. It meant a greater chance for a full recovery and possibility of having more children at another time. The only con was that it meant destroying her baby, yet that con outweighed all the pros in her mind.

She found herself asking, "Why me?" despite herself. She knew the answer, "Why not me?" Why had she been so blessed with a loving husband, two beautiful children, a home and a stable income when so many others didn't have these? Why should she escape the hardships others who were far worthier than her experienced? She had been blessed for so long and she believed she would continue to be blessed despite her fears for herself, her children, her future.

"Fear not," the words of the angel to Mary echoed in her spirit. She clung to those words.

When her Oncotype score came back indicating a moderate likelihood of recurrence, they decided to go ahead with chemo followed by a lumpectomy. After the baby's birth they would evaluate whether to pursue further surgery or radiation.

"I would like to be able to nurse this baby at least for a while if at all possible," Joy had stated to Dale and her doctor, thus making her case for the lumpectomy. So the course had been set.

Josh and Scott helped clear away the dishes after dinner.

"Josh and Scott, take Ashley and Jacob into the front room so the adults can talk," Esther told them. "You can put in a video for the little kids while you work on your homework."

"Oh, grandma, do I have to?" Scott had complained.

"Come on, Scott," Josh said, not allowing Scott to say anything more. He escorted Scott and the others out of the room.

"Josh is such a good kid," Joy commented once they left.

"Yes, both of them are blessings," Esther said as she poured coffee for them. "So what's on your minds?"

Dale looked over at Joy before proceeding. "Mom, we have a difficult situation." He didn't say he had bad news lest he upset his mom too much, but he also wanted to prepare her for what they would say.

"What could be so difficult? The baby is healthy, my grandchildren are healthy, work is steady. After losing your dad and your sister and my job I can handle pretty much anything."

"Mom, grandpa," Dale made sure to include his grandfather in the discussion, "Joy has breast cancer."

"Oh no," Esther said, sitting down. She had been prepared for anything but that. "What are you going to do?"

"There are some things we can do, without hurting the baby. Joy's going to start chemo then have a lumpectomy if all goes well. There are some drugs Joy can take that are not supposed to cross the placenta so the baby should be okay."

"How bad is the cancer?" Esther asked. "Did they catch it in time?"

"It's a fairly aggressive form but we have every reason to believe it will be okay. Once the baby is born Joy can continue chemotherapy if necessary and maybe undergo radiation."

"But that's five months from now. What if it grows quickly?"

"That's a what-if, mom," Joy jumped in. "We can't make decisions on what-ifs, only on what we know. Radiation will definitely hurt the baby, as will aggressive use of chemo. Why take the chance of harming the baby for a what-if?"

"But if something happens to you . . ." Esther didn't want to finish the thought. They all knew where it was heading. Two more grandchildren without a mother. No, that can't happen, she mustn't let it happen, Esther thought, but it was out of her hands.

"We'll be okay, mom," Dale assured her, much as his dad, Dale Sr., had assured her when their babies had been born. Much as she had assured Dale, Jr., each time hardship had entered their life, first losing his dad then all of the trouble with his sister. Now it was his turn to assure her.

"Have you thought this out? Yes, aggressive treatment would hurt the baby, but you have two other children who are little more than babies to think about." There, she had said it. She had to say it even if the decision had already been made. She had to speak her piece.

"We'll be fine. I'll be fine. I don't know why God is allowing this to happen but I'm trusting in him to get us through," Joy said.

"God, where was God when Dale's dad died, leaving you two children without a father? God didn't prevent that, why will he prevent this? They say God will never give us more than we can handle, still God doesn't pull his punches either, does he? Life sure has a way of knocking us down," Esther surprised herself at her comments.

"And when it does, you always helped pull me back up, mom" Dale said. "We will get through this together, with the grace of God."

Esther knew where Dale had gotten his faith. She had always been the first to trust in God, but this was too much, her beautiful daughter-in-law and that unborn baby. What if they lost both of them? How would Dale hold up? How would she hold up? Would this be the last straw to knock her off balance from the high-wire she had been balancing on ever since Dale's death? What if the what-if came true?

"I can tell you've made up your mind so I guess there's nothing more to say. I guess all we can do is pray." The words sounded hollow in her ears, but she felt she had to say them anyway. "Do you need help with the kids or with doctor appointments, or anything?"

"Thanks, mom, I knew we could count on you. We are doing okay right now. We might need the extra help once Joy begins treatment. Joy's mom has also offered to help. We'll let you know if we need your help before then. Right now, just having your prayers means a lot."

"You know you always have that," Esther assured them.

"And mine, too. I may not be much good at chasing kids but I can certainly pray," her dad had been quietly watching the scene play out before him, unsure what to say, not wanting to intrude as he watched his daughter experience yet another heartache. He stood up and squeezed Esther's shoulders then hugged Joy, patting her belly. "We'll keep both of you safe," he said.

Joy had been relieved to have that conversation over with. She smiled over at Dale during the drive home, the kids sleeping in the back.

"Well, that wasn't too bad," she commented.

"No, not at all. I had thought mom might have put up more of a fight."

Joy was relieved that had not happened, yet a little worried. Had some of the fight gone out of her mother-in-law, she wondered. No time to worry about it right now, she told herself, still it troubled her. She had been inspired by Esther's drive, how she had managed to raise her children as a single parent. How she had dealt with Dale's sister and her problems and how she was now raising those kids. She was a strong woman. Joy admired that in her.

Her own mother had none of that drive. She never would have been able to handle it if anything had happened to dad. Perhaps that's why nothing had happened. God gives us challenges according to our ability to deal with those challenges, right? Maybe if she had been more like her mother, God wouldn't have dealt her such a hand, Joy thought with a sigh. Maybe if she were weaker . . . Instead God was making her stronger, growing her faith. She tried to comfort herself with that thought, but it was little comfort. She didn't really know what God was up to. She hoped God knew what he was doing because she didn't.

Joy's parents had been supportive of their decision. For some reason, instead of feeling good about this, she had been a little put off.

"Of course you can't do anything that would hurt that precious baby inside you. God will provide," her mother had asserted.

Easy for her to say, she had thought. You're not the one whose life was on the line, who could lose both of her babies through death. She didn't know why she found herself irritated with her mom. She wanted to explode at her. Displaced anger, she thought, easier to get angry at her mom than the doctor who held her baby and her life in his hands, or at God. Anger, the second stage of Kubler-Ross' five stages of dying. But she wasn't dying, she told herself. She was just dealing with cancer, not a death sentence.

There was a time when the diagnosis of cancer was a death sentence but not now with all of the new treatments available. Many survived. She had seen them at the Relay for Life in support of the

American Cancer Society each year. However there also were all of the luminaries that lined the walk representing those who had died. Maybe this was just another form of denial; after all, we are all under a death sentence while on this earth, some go earlier than others, Joy told herself.

Joy was familiar with the Kubler-Ross stages of dying. Some days she lived in denial. Who can confront death every day? She pretended the diagnosis had never happened and her life was back to normal. Other times she bargained with God. Just save my baby, she would say. Get me through this without hurting my baby and I'll do anything you want. She had no idea what acceptance, the final stage, looked like.

Her mom's faith seemed so easy. Joy didn't like that. Had her mom ever had doubts, questioned God or the church? And what about her dad? She knew her mom questioned her dad at times, still overall he ruled, his decision reigned supreme in their home except for those few occasions when her mom had stood up to him.

No, she liked Esther's faith more than her mom's. It was more real. She liked the fact that Esther didn't have any easy answers for her. There were no easy answers when two lives were on the line the way her life and her baby's life were. There were no easy answers when confronted with the big C – cancer, or the big D – death. She guessed she trusted God, but only so far. She wondered if God would catch her if she were to let go, give up on this balancing act she called her life. Sometimes it seemed like it would be so easy to do that, to just give up, call it quits, allow herself to sink into a fog of depression and never come out, or at least not until this baby was born, but then there were Ashley and Jacob, depending on her, and there was Dale, loving her, and so she found she had reason to get through another day, more than reason enough.

"You okay?" Dale looked over at her. "You're awfully quiet."

"Just tired," she said. "It will be good to get home and get to bed." She couldn't share these thoughts with Dale, didn't want to burden him any more than he already was. No, she couldn't share these. They were for her and her God.

"I'll put the kids to bed," he told her when they got home. "You rest." This time she didn't fight him. She was glad to take him up on his offer, welcoming the comfort of sleep.

Chemo was scheduled to start immediately, ending during the eighth month of pregnancy.

"One possibility we do need to be aware of is early delivery. While there is no evidence that the chemo hurts the baby, there are incidents of premature labor," her doctor warned.

Joy had wanted to reject the whole deal when told that. Even though she had read it on one of the websites she had researched, it sounded so much more real coming from a live doctor sitting in front of her. She had been looking for an excuse to call the whole thing off.

"Then let's not do this," she exclaimed, starting to get up.

Dale kept her from leaving, lightly placing his arm on her thigh, quietly reassuring her.

"That's okay, we are aware of it. We have talked about it," he looked over at Joy to get her affirmation, then proceeded. "So when do we begin?"

They scheduled a time to put a port into her body for delivering the chemo.

"This is a better way to get the chemo in your system," she had been told when she questioned the need for it. The surgery to place the port had been fairly easy. They had used a local anesthesia and had sent her home that same day with instructions to keep it dry and safe for forty-eight hours. She experienced minimal pain and no complications. She wished the same could have been said about the chemo which she started the next week. She had read that some experience little negative reaction to chemo; however she wasn't among their number.

The reprieve from the nausea of the first trimester of her pregnancy was short lived as she experienced renewed bouts with nausea after starting treatment, but what was worse was the exhaustion. It was tiring enough just being pregnant as her body did the work of nurturing a new life. The additional burden of chemotherapy left her with no energy for anything, much less the care of two small children and a job. She was glad she had made her decisions about treatment options before chemo had begun because now she walked around in a chemo-induced fog. Nothing tasted the same or smelled the same. She couldn't make the simplest of decisions and yet she had to. Somehow she forced herself to keep going.

When her hair began to fall out, she asked her mother-in-law to shave it off rather than endure prolonging the inevitable. She had opted against a wig, preferring to wrap her head in a scarf like she had often done while dancing. That was the more comfortable option, she thought, wondering if she would ever be comfortable in her own body again.

Chapter 15

Sara felt so small and self-centered after talking to Joy. What were her problems in comparison to what Joy was dealing with?

"Do you want me to come home and help?"

"Don't be silly. Finish school. I've got plenty of help between mom and Dale's mom and the women at church."

"Well, at least let me stay with you over spring break."

"Don't you have any plans for a fun spring break at Daytona Beach? This is your senior year. You should make the most of it."

"And I will, by spending it with you. Besides, you know mom and dad would never pay for a 'senior spring break.'"

"Maybe I was just hoping to live vicariously through you. You know, revisit those carefree, kid-free days of my youth."

"Were they that 'care-free?' Because if they were, I want to know how you did it."

"No, I guess not, each life stage has its own challenges. Still it's nice to fantasize. You wouldn't deprive a girl of that, would you?"

"So, it's set," Sara ignored her sister's comment. "I'll stay with you over spring break," she insisted. She had actually hoped for an excuse to quit school or at least to take a leave of absence. She was hard into senior slump, just wanting it to be over. She was finding it hard to keep up with what needed to be done before graduation. The whole situation with Jeff had complicated her life. The incident with Craig had been just that, an incident, one she wasn't ready to repeat with someone else. She had been using Craig as a rebound. It was awkward. She couldn't entirely avoid running into him, but at least now he seemed as determined to avoid her as she was to avoid him. It made it easier.

At least she had her art to throw herself into. She was beefing up her portfolio. She didn't know why. It wasn't as if she was going on to the Chicago Institute of Art as she had once dreamed of doing, or anywhere else. It wasn't as if she would be able to use it for a job. It just felt right. She could lose herself in her art, yet at the same time find herself as her personal struggles came out in her artwork. She found herself doing self-portraits, sketches and oil paintings of a woman torn apart, pulled in different directions and not knowing which way to go. Immobilized by the tension of competing demands, her favorite drawing showed two heads connected at the top by hair, an elongated view running horizontally or vertically depending on whether she felt she was standing on her head or lying down, somewhat at rest. It was a mirror image that spoke to her in her confusion.

After talking to Joy, a picture of her sister began to form in her brain. She drew Joy, the ballerina, yet round with child, struggling to pirouette with the extra weight. Then she drew her, her head wrapped in a turban to mask her hair loss. She experimented with what her beautiful older sister would look like as she dealt with breast cancer. All the more reason why she needed to be there with her, Sara thought. She let images flow. She wasn't sure exactly what she was drawing, perhaps a series of sketches in preparation for an oil painting. She had some vague image in her brain, waiting to take shape in order to come to life on canvas.

Spring break at Joy's had been just what she needed. She came back with renewed images and ideas for drawing. She still had classes to finish before graduation and then there was the pressure to find a job, have a plan, know what she was going to do after graduation. Her dad didn't want to find out that he had wasted his hard-earned money on art.

"Ease off, dad," Joy had told him over spring break while over at their parents' home. "Give her some time. How many twenty somethings this day know what they want to be doing with their life?"

"You did, your brothers did."

"I only wanted to dance, and I'm grateful I had the opportunity to do so. Maybe Sara is meant to be an artist."

"At least you have a husband to support you."

"I didn't when I was Sara's age. And as far as the boys, well, they never had much imagination anyway. And besides, that was then, fifteen years ago. Times have changed." Sara had appreciated Joy's support more than Joy knew. It was good to have someone on her side, pulling for her, especially as she was feeling pulled apart.

Sara had told Joy about Craig. "I feel so foolish," she had stated.

"Sara, if that's the only foolish thing you did while in college, I would consider you the brightest girl I know. That was nothing."

"But I keep wondering, what's wrong with me that I find the wrong guy all the time?"

"There's nothing wrong with you, nothing that most people deal with as they struggle to find themselves and find love."

"You didn't. You dated Dale in high school."

"Yes, we dated, but then there were those eight years while I was with the Ballet and he was starting his business. We weren't exclusive. Do you think we never dated anyone else?"

"That was the impression I had."

"No, we each dated other people. There were long stretches of time when I was away and we didn't see each other, but every time we did, every time I came home or he came to visit, it was as if we had never been apart. With a few rough edges here and there, we would pick up wherever we left off. The other people we dated just helped us clarify what we didn't want."

"I wish I could find someone like that."

"You will, Sara, just give it time." Joy had assured her but Sara found it hard to believe.

"What are you drawing? Mind if I look?"

"I do mind," Sara started to say then saw the young man from New Year's Eve. "Larry, right?"

"Yes, and you're still Sara."

"Yes, I am," Sara laughed.

"So, are you going to let me see?" Sara had instinctively covered the sketch she was working on. She was seated at her favorite spot in the Union, facing away from the students, a cup of coffee at her side as she gazed out the window, sometimes lost in thought, other times busy sketching or studying. It beat the library. Sometimes she found the silence of the library oppressive. She enjoyed the hum of voices about her as long as she wasn't required to participate.

"I don't know. What will you give me for the privilege?"

"Hmmm, playing hard to get. Okay, how about a coffee refill?"

"Sure," Sara said and handed him her cup.

He came back with two coffees and sat down beside her. "So how come you didn't call me?" he asked.

"You wanted me to call you?"

"Why do you think I gave you my number?"

"I thought that was for if my computer crashed."

"That too, but primarily it was a ruse. Since I can't enchant you with my looks I thought I would use my geek skills to tantalize you. Apparently they failed with you."

"Actually, I took a shower and it washed off before I had a chance to write it down."

"Well, I won't make the same mistake twice." He reached for her sketch pad and wrote his name and phone number on the inside cover.

"There, now you'll have no excuse. So what were you working on so intently?"

"Just sketching. Pictures of my sister." He thumbed through the pictures.

"Nice, she's beautiful."

"Yes, she is."

"Is she dating anyone?" he asked, raising an eyebrow.

"She's married. Don't you see she's pregnant?"

"Rats, then what about you? Are you dating anyone?"

"No, not at the moment."

"More good news for me."

"Maybe," she said with a smile. He finished his coffee then got up.

"I have to get to class. You've got my number. Use it."

"How about you call me?" Sara replied as she grabbed his hand and wrote her number on it. "Now, don't wash that."

"Never," he said as he kissed his hand in salute. Two minutes later her cell phone rang.

"It's Larry. Just putting your number into my contacts and calling you so you can do the same. Catch you later."

"Nice sketches," a familiar voice said as she sat once again along the Red Cedar. Had it only been a year since she had gotten engaged? Didn't seem possible, so much had happened since then. This time Jeff sat down next to her, no hug, no kisses. He seemed a little subdued, unlike him, at least not how she remembered him.

"What's up? I'm glad you called," Jeff asked.

"Are you? Are you really? After how I treated you?"

"What about how I treated you?"

"You didn't mean to hurt me, I realize that."

"But is that an excuse? Sounds like a convenient justification for many well-intentioned mistakes we make."

"Maybe," Sara paused, "I know I didn't respond kindly last time we talked."

"That's okay. I wasn't expecting forgiveness."

"Would you just let me say I'm sorry so I can get this over with," Sara said with a smile. "You always were exasperating."

"And you loved it."

"Yes, I did. I loved you. Look, Jeff, I'm sorry I wasn't more understanding of you, what you were struggling with."

"Apology accepted, as long as you forgive me and say we can still be friends."

"You drive a hard bargain."

"Take it or leave it."

"I'll take it." It felt so good, so natural, being with Jeff. No wonder she had fallen for him. "I've missed this, talking to you."

"Well, you've no one to blame but yourself for that." Sara closed her sketch book and hit Jeff with it.

"Let's get out of here. You want pizza?" Jeff asked.

"I'm always good for pizza," she responded as they both stood up.

Chapter 16

Joy was relieved to have the recital over with. Time to start planning for next year, she thought, after a break to have this baby. She always enjoyed the recital and looked forward to it almost as much as the kids, still she was also glad when it was done. Fortunately it was nowhere as big a production as the one put on by the other dance studio in town, her main competitor. In comparison hers was but a minor blip. Her focus was on ballet and to that end she only had eight classes she offered. Some ran twice a week, others only once a week, such as the beginning classes for pre-school aged children. She offered two such classes, one on Monday and one on Wednesday. On the opposite days she offered beginner classes for grade K through second in the same time slot. After that the classes were based on how far along the students were in ballet, whether a beginner, intermediate or advanced. Intermediate and advanced met twice a week. Those preparing for toe shoes had to practice a minimum of twice a week in order to gain the strength they needed to go "on pointe."

She avoided the necessity of eight different routines, one for each class, through combining some classes with the more advanced, doing what they could and the younger being given easier dance routines. She felt this allowed her to do more with less. She was able to combine the two pre-school classes and the two K through second grade classes into one dance for each. Parents who had children enrolled in both sections of their age group were thereby allowed to purchase just one costume rather than two, something they appreciated. The recital included two routines for the youngest children and three routines involving the beginners through advanced. Because hers was a small school, she didn't have a large class of students in toe shoes. Sometimes she would feature them with a solo routine amidst the other dancers. She also usually scheduled a Christmas recital that was not as developed as the spring one but gave the children a chance to perform and experience the joy of dancing before an audience in preparation for the spring recital.

She found that doing this helped the children feel more at ease when the spring recital came around.

There were times when Joy was envious of the other dance studio that had hundreds of students and had a much larger offering of classes, including jazz, tap and combination classes besides ballet. She would have had to find someone to teach those classes, would have incurred a much greater workload which would have required more management on her part. No, she was content to focus on ballet, at least for now. She had assistants to teach the pre-school and K through second grade classes and taught the beginners, intermediate and advanced classes herself with assistants.

She was able to get to know her forty to fifty students and enjoyed giving them individual attention, something she wouldn't have been able to do with more students. She also was able to get to know many of the parents that dropped off their children or waited and watched each class. They had become a large, extended family. She had able teenage assistants ready to take over when the effort to stay balanced with a large protruding belly proved too much for her. She roamed about the room, adjusting postures, making corrections until she needed to sit and prop up her swelling feet. The remnants of the chemo she had received and her pregnancy left her light-headed at times. Her feet would swell throughout the day till she could barely slip them into her ballet slippers. Still, when everyone was gone, she would slip them back on, wrap her belly in a gauzy swathe and attempt to put herself through her paces.

"What are you doing?" Esther asked her when she saw a light on in the practice room.

"I don't want to lose my ability to dance," Joy replied. "I'm trying to keep toned as much as possible."

"There will be plenty of time for that after the baby is born."

"No, there won't, you know that. Then I'll be busy with the baby and surgery. I'll lose it all if I don't keep up now. Use it or lose it. Besides, the doctor said the best thing I could do was to keep moving."

"Give yourself a break, Joy, Don't be so hard on yourself."

"I'm not being hard on myself," Joy insisted – but she knew the lie of what she was saying. She just didn't want to give up so easily, didn't want to give up on dancing. She was afraid that if she stopped pushing herself she would come to a complete halt and never get up again. She was afraid that if she stopped she would give up. She loved to dance.

"Just a few minutes, mom, just give me a few minutes," she asked. Esther corralled her grandkids in order to give Joy her few minutes.

"Come on, kids. Let mommy dance. I think there are some cookies left," she told them as they went back to the office.

Esther had started helping out in the office a few months ago. It had seemed like the least she could. She was good with numbers even though she had never gone beyond high school math. Basic bookkeeping didn't require an advanced degree in math, just the ability to keep numbers straight, and with the computer, she didn't even have to be able to add and subtract, just had to enter numbers correctly. Joy's operation was not that big, so Esther was able to take it over without a lot of trouble. This freed Joy to focus more on the actual teaching, which she loved. She also helped with her grandkids, freeing Joy to focus more on her pregnancy.

Esther still wasn't sure what she wanted to do with what was left of her life. She had worked in food services all of her working life. She wasn't sure she wanted to keep doing that yet she didn't have any training for anything else. She was thinking about going back to school, maybe get an associate's degree from the local community college, but hadn't determined what classes she wanted to take. She was enjoying doing the books for Joy. Perhaps that could be a new career, she thought. She needed to get better at computers. She knew how to send and receive emails and how to search the Internet for information. She was learning how to use Excel and how to manage data bases from helping in the office. She had taken some basic computing classes through the library and of course Josh was a wealth of information about computers.

Despite Josh's good nature and patience, he often ended up just doing what she needed on the computer rather than teaching her how to do it herself. No, she needed to learn more, she told herself, and so was considering taking some basic computer classes on spreadsheets and analytics, but right now she was content with what she was doing. She had received an extension on her unemployment benefits and thought that maybe God had given her this time to be available to help her son and his family. Josh and Scott were able to take care of themselves to a large extent with supervision by her dad. They still needed attention, but not like Ashley and Jacob. They were old enough to be left on their own and if something came up, her dad was there to help. She felt this was her time, her chance to get to know her daughter-in-law better.

She put aside her fears for the future: Would she be able to get another job? What about Joy? What about Kathleen, her errant daughter? She put these aside for the moment to focus on the moment, what life was bringing her right now. When she thought about the future her head spun. Worries enough for the day, she told herself, no sense in buying troubles from tomorrow.

"Ready?" Esther asked as Joy joined her and her kids in the office, out of her ballet clothes and in her street clothes.

"Ready," she stated. She seemed so calm, Esther thought. Dance had a way of doing that for her, Esther had noticed. It was a form of meditation, or so it appeared. Joy always seemed calmer after having some time for herself to stretch and dance. Like yoga for others. She wished she had a similar outlet.

"Joy, did you ever consider teaching an adult class?"

"No, why, you interested?"

"Or maybe exercise classes for pregnant women?" Esther's brain was bursting with ideas. "I bet there would be a market for that."

Joy laughed. "Maybe, but right now I've got all I can handle. Come on, kids," she gathered her children. "Are you done?"

"Yes, time to go home, see what damage Josh and Scott have done to the house. Do you think they'll have dinner ready?" That was one disadvantage of helping at the dance studio--the hours interfered with dinner time. Classes started immediately after school and ended by seven most days, including individual sessions Joy scheduled. It didn't give her any time to fix dinner. Still it wasn't a bad schedule. At least it got her home at a decent hour.

"I'm sure they found the pizza delivery number," Joy laughed. "And if you're lucky, they saved you some." She took Ashley and Jacob by the hand. "Come on, let's see what daddy has for us. You could join us," she said to Esther. "I don't know what Dale has fixed but whatever it is, you're welcome to share it," Joy offered.

"No, thank you, another time. I have to get home." Esther didn't spend every week night at the studio. There wasn't enough to keep her busy. Besides she needed to be looking for employment in order to keep her unemployment. It was getting harder to find positions she was qualified for that she hadn't already applied for. She also didn't like leaving Josh and Scott under her dad's supervision every day. They still needed her time and attention and her cooking if nothing else.

She thought about the idea of adult classes on her way home. Joy already had the space, owned the building, why not use it more, add day time classes? The idea intrigued her. She could help market the classes. She had friends who might be interested.

She sighed when she got home and saw the state the kitchen had been left in. At least they must have fixed themselves something to eat, she thought. The boys were sitting in front of the TV with her dad, eating mac and cheese with hot dogs, Scott's favorite. Must have been his night to pick the meal.

"Where're your vegetables?" Esther questioned, sneaking up on them. They jumped.

"Sorry, grandma, I didn't realize it was so late. We'll clean the kitchen at the next commercial."

"What are you watching?"

"Baseball."

"Is it that time already? Seems like we just finished basketball season," Esther commented. "Did you leave any for me?" she asked as she sat down.

"Sure, grandma, I'll get you some," Josh jumped up to get Esther a plate.

"There's always something on ESPN," her dad commented.

"No homework?" Esther asked as she took a fork full from the plate Josh had delivered.

"All done. Only one more week of school left. How's Aunt Joy?"

That's right, Esther remembered. This was the last week of dance classes. There were celebrations for the finish of the year scheduled.

Joy's baby was due soon. There had been some talk of having a C-section once the baby was large enough to survive on its own in order to begin more aggressive treatment as soon as possible, but Joy had nixed that idea as well.

"We've come this far, I want to give my baby the best chance possible , which means waiting for when God determines it's time.

The longer the baby stays in the womb, the better the chance for a healthy baby. We've come this far by faith, why stop now?" Joy had insisted. "Besides, I want to wait until after the recital is over." Now that the recital was over, Joy figured God could begin the labor process any time now, or so she had told Esther.

"She's good."

"No baby yet?"

"No baby," Esther replied as she relaxed into her chair.

Chapter 17

"Let me get a picture of you and your dad," Sara's mom insisted. Students in green garb were everywhere, rushing to and from graduation ceremonies. Parents, grandparents, other family members sauntered here and there, ready for this long awaited event in their child's life. There were multiple ceremonies scheduled at different times on the campus, orchestrated to accommodate the large number of students, too large to fit into one building. Sara hadn't wanted to participate in the graduation ceremony but her decision had been vetoed by her dad.

"I want to see my baby girl graduate from college," he had asserted.

"You won't be able to see much. I'll just be one of thousands."

"That's okay. I'll know you are there. I didn't pay all of this money to put you through school to just have it end with no recognition." Sara had no option but to agree and make the best of it.

"Sara, hi!" Jeff came up beside her and gave her a hug followed by his parents.

"Sara, good to see you," Jeff's mom and dad each gave her a hug as well.

"Mom, dad, you remember Jeff's parents?"

"Good to see you again, and you too, young man." Sara's dad shook Jeff's and his dad's hands and kissed Jeff's mom on the cheek. Her mother just said, hi, as Jeff's dad hugged her.

"Awkward," Sara mumbled under her breath.

"Here, let me take a picture of you with your parents." Jeff took the camera away from Sara's mom and posed them for a picture. Sara was relieved to see Anne heading their way.

"Hey, Sara, we've got to get going."

"Not before I get a picture of you three graduates together," Jeff's father said as he snapped a picture.

Jeff and his parents said goodbye amid another round of hugs.

"Come and see us sometime," Jeff's mother said as she hugged Sara. "You're always welcome."

"Thank you, I'll do that," Sara replied as they left. She felt a tap on her shoulder and turned around to see Larry.

"You look great," he said as he kissed her cheek. "I've only got a minute, have to make it to my graduation ceremony. See you tonight?"

"I'll call you," Sara said as he took off.

"Who was that?" her mom asked.

"Oh, just a friend," she responded.

"Now we really have to be going," Anne said and pulled her away.

"See you after graduation," Sara said to her parents. "Thanks for rescuing me," she told Anne once they were out of earshot.

"You owe me."

"That I do," said with a laugh. "Come on, let's graduate from this place."

The floor of the Kresge Center was a mass of green and white with disembodied heads bobbing above the sea of green. Sara's parents had no idea where their daughter was from their vantage point in the stands.

"That was rude," her dad commented.

"What was?" her mom feigned surprise.

"You, how you treated Jeff and his parents. Just because they are no longer engaged doesn't mean you have to be rude. You hardly said a word to them."

"Look," Mary said, distracting her husband, "do you think that's Sara over there." She pointed to a corner along the side of the floor as the ceremony began.

Chapter 18

"You know, I'm not an invalid," Joy insisted, yet she was glad for her sister's company. "The way all of you hover over me, you'd think I was on death's door not undergoing a normal life function." Sara had moved back home after graduation and had moved into Joy's home to watch Ashley and Jacob while Joy had her baby. Joy appreciated the help, but also felt uncomfortable with all of the attention, not just from her mom but from her mother-in-law and now her sister.

Sara's visit during spring break brought a welcome relief. It had been good to forget some about cancer as she had laughed with her little sister. These brief vacations were needed respite from the all-consuming nature of cancer. Some days it felt like she lived, ate and breathed cancer. Despite her tiredness she had been grateful to go to the studio each day and lose herself in dance. Despite her dizziness and nausea from the chemo, she still found time to stretch, meditate and dance. She relished watching the young dancers. At home, she spent what little energy she had on her children, allowing housework to pile up under the watchful eye of Esther and her mom who breezed in each week, trying to restore some order to the chaos that was her life on chemo. Through it all she had kept going, spurred on by her desire, no her need, to keep going for the sake of her little ones, not just Ashley and Jacob, but baby Grace, growing inside her.

They had not wanted to know the sex of the baby, had wanted to be surprised, but with all of the tests she had been undergoing, one of the technicians had let slip with a she. Joy found that she wasn't upset after all. It felt good to be able to put a name and gender on their faceless baby cohabiting in the same body with her.

"This one is a fighter, look at her kicking," the technician had said at one of her ultra-sounds.

That's good, Joy had thought. Fight, Gracie. I need you to fight with me. I need you to fight for me. She felt they were in this together. They had decided to call her Grace because that was what she was to them, a grace.

It had been a relief to quit chemo just in time for the year-end recital. What hadn't been a relief was the last visit to the oncologist.

"It appears the mass hasn't shrunk enough to do a lumpectomy. Because of this I'm recommending a mastectomy. Perhaps a double mastectomy. It's hard to monitor this particular form of cancer. There is a chance of there being breast cancer present but undetected in the other breast. Sometimes it's better to remove both breasts because of this. We can schedule it for a month after the baby is born." Joy had felt the same clutch in her chest she had experienced when the diagnosis had first been decreed: a sharp pain and clenching in her chest like she couldn't breathe. "Breathe, breathe," she told herself, "This too will pass."

She didn't say anything in response to what the doctor had said. "We'll talk it over and let you know," Dale had said. She remained quiet while driving home.

"You want to talk?" Dale asked gently.

"No, not now," she responded.

"What's wrong," Esther asked when they came home. "Bad news?" She wanted to know and didn't want to know. Sara came in from the front room where she had been keeping the kids occupied.

"You go lie down," Dale told Joy, who gratefully escaped to her bedroom.

"The chemo hasn't worked as well as we had hoped," he told them. Esther didn't know what to say, they had been so hopeful.

"What are you going to do?"

"I guess a mastectomy after the baby is born, then radiation."

"Dale, I'm so sorry."

"I know, mom. We really appreciate all of your help, but right now I think we need some time to ourselves to figure things out. Sara, could you make sure the kids have something to eat?"

"Dinner's in the oven," Esther said as she hugged Dale and left.

Dale was surprised when Joy came back downstairs.

"What are you doing?"

"I'm going to be having a baby. I'm going to spend time with my other babies and then I'm going to have this baby and then we'll go from there," she said as she called the children for dinner.

"And the mastectomy?"

"We can talk about that later," she said as Sara came in with the children.

Chapter 19

"I'm fine," she kept insisting. Everybody needs to get a life she said to herself, not out loud. She didn't mean it, appreciated the help but sometimes it was suffocating. It was a relief when the labor pains finally started, signaling the onset of delivery. It was a relief to be in the car with Dale.

"Just the two of us," she said with a smile, reaching over and placing her hand on Dale's arm.

"That's right, just you and me, kid," Dale replied. "We haven't had much time together lately, have we?"

"I'll be glad when we get back into a normal routine, whatever that is."

"That's the price for being so loved," he smiled. All week long, phone calls came from both of their moms and church members. They all wanted to know how Joy was doing. "We'll let Sara handle all the phone calls now. For now it's just you and me, but that won't be long," he said, glancing at her belly. "Just you and me and baby Grace." They had decided on a Scripture based name, in keeping with her family tradition. Ashley had been an exception. Joy had always liked the name, had wanted to change her name to Ashley when she was six and so had determined the next best thing was to name her daughter Ashley and let her daughter live with it. Since then she opted for the simplicity of Biblical names. There were so many names out there to choose from, some strange to her ears. She figured she couldn't go wrong with tried and true names from the Bible.

She smiled at Dale then gasped as the next contraction caught her off guard. "Little Grace seems to be in a hurry to get here."

"We'll get there in time," Dale assured her as he stepped up his speed. Better to err on the side of caution, get there early, rather than too late, he told himself as he focused on driving safely to the hospital.

Joy wasn't worried about the delivery. She had done this before. It was what waited for her after the delivery that concerned her. But that was for then, for now she was having a baby.

Joy was escorted out of the hospital in a wheelchair, little Grace in her arms. The birth had been relatively routine, if a birth could ever be routine. Each birth was as different as the couple and the baby being born.

She was worn-out, yet content. The baby was healthy. That had been all she cared about. Her doctor wanted to schedule her surgery as soon as possible, just giving her enough time to recuperate and regain most of her strength before assaulting her with surgery but she was reluctant to agree to this. She wanted to be able to breast-feed her baby, even if for a short time. The colostrum would provide important immunities to her baby. Besides she wanted to enjoy her breasts as long as she could before losing them forever. She knew she could put off surgery for a while but would have to comply eventually.

Now that she had safely delivered her baby, the reality of what was yet to come hit home. They would give her something to dry up her breasts to make surgery easier. She had asked for months, been given weeks to breast-feed her baby before weaning her. It wasn't optimal to her thinking but it was workable. She would make it work. After so many months of fighting with doctors, she wasn't going to just cave in, was she? Part of her was tired of fighting. She had done what she had set out to do: She had safely brought her baby to full term. What happened next was inconsequential, she was inconsequential in the wider scheme of things or so she thought as she gazed down at this precious child.

"I choose you, child, I choose you to live. Now you must live, I can no longer do it for you. It's up to you."

Chapter 20

The reality of her sister's cancer was different now that she was up close and personal. It had been easy to romanticize from the distance of school. Now that she was home, spending time with her sister and her family, the situation was all too real and it wasn't pretty. Throwing up because you are pregnant was different from throwing up due to the chemicals being poured into her body whose purpose was to kill. The difference lay in the reason behind the nausea.

Suffering is pain without meaning, she had read somewhere. People will accept much pain if they know there is a reason behind it, but they won't suffer for long. The pain of childbirth is alleviated by the reason behind the pain. The meaning behind the pain Joy was now experiencing was that she was fighting for her life, yet Joy didn't seem to get it. Since her daughter's birth, Joy seemed to have lost her will to live.

Post-partum depression, yet more than that. All Joy had been living for during the past months was to give birth to a healthy baby. Now that that had occurred there was the natural let-down that occurs any time you reach an important goal. She needed a new reason to keep going. Joy took some comfort in holding her baby but other than that she seemed lifeless.

Her mother-in-law had noticed it too. Sara had met Esther at Joy and Dale's wedding. She had been a junior bridesmaid, being twelve. Esther hadn't been more than a passing acquaintance until recently, first during spring break when she had stayed with Joy and now. They sat in the kitchen while Joy and the baby napped and the other kids watched a video.

"It's completely normal to experience some post-partum depression after having a baby. It's also normal to be depressed when you're dealing with cancer. The problem is, I think both have hit at the same time for Joy. But she's a trooper. She'll pull out of it," Esther had reassured Sara with a confidence she herself didn't feel.

What if she doesn't pull out of this soon? She would need all of her strength, physical, emotional, and spiritual for the challenges ahead. She couldn't go into surgery like this, Esther had worried. It just wasn't like Joy. Joy had become a true daughter to her over the years that she and Dale had dated and since their marriage. She remembered a laughing, young teenager on the brink of womanhood, sitting in her kitchen and joking with Dale while she fixed dinner.

"Staying for dinner?" she had asked.

"Only if you are asking," Joy had responded.

"You're always welcome. You know that." She had been more of a daughter than her own daughter.

Esther paused as she went through the mail. An envelope with that all-too-familiar hand writing was hidden among the bills. Kathleen, Esther thought. She hadn't heard from her for a while. No news is good news, she had told herself. So what does this mean, she wondered.

They had had little contact over the past five years. At first she had written more often and Esther had arranged visits for the kids. Kathleen would call whenever she had a chance, tripling Esther's phone bill.

She had made every effort to keep the kids in her daughter's life until she realized that every time they saw their mother there was a setback. She didn't know all that went on during the visits or on the phone, she just knew that afterwards the kids would act out and it would take her days, if not weeks, to get them settled back down. It seemed she was paying twice over for her daughter's poor choices.

It had not been a hard adjustment for the boys to their mother's being gone as they had been living with Esther since birth. She had taken care of them whenever Kathleen wasn't able to for whatever reason. So in some ways it had been easy, but was it ever easy where kids are concerned? Their mother still had a hold over them. Esther could see that. Even after she had been given full custody, Kathleen had a hold over them. It didn't matter what the courts said. So, out of the best interest for the kids, she had started making the time between visits longer and longer until they were non-existent. She finally had to put a stop to phone calls as well. Besides being expensive, the cost in terms of emotional turmoil for the kids was too much.

"Mom says you need to send her more money," Josh had told her after one such call.

"What?"

"Yeah, she says then she would write us more often."

Esther knew that excuse. The money would be used for cigarettes or whatever else they used as currency in prison. "She also wants to know when we will be visiting again," he added.

"We'll see," Esther said, putting him off. She felt a pang of guilt. Who was she to keep him from his mother? At seven he couldn't see how his mom was trying to use him to get Esther to do stuff for her. How little she had changed, Esther had thought.

The next time Kathleen had called she had told her she wasn't to use Josh to get what she wanted. "If you need money, you talk to me. If you want us to visit, you make arrangements with me. Don't put Josh in the middle."

"They're my kids. I can say what I want to say."

"No, that's not what the court says. I have legal custody, not you."

"They are still my kids. Nothing can change that." After one too many such exchanges Esther had decided to cut off contact. She sent cards at Christmas and on Kathleen's birthday, but nothing other than that. Kathleen for her part sent the occasional letters and Christmas cards to the kids. On their birthday and Christmas, Esther always bought the boys a present from their mom. No kids deserved to go without on their birthday or Christmas she had told herself. Josh had long since figured out that the gifts from his mom were actually from his grandmother, but he didn't let on to Scott who still thought they were from her.

She had done it for them, she told herself, but now and then guilt would sneak in. Was it really for them or was it for her? Had she cut off contact with their mom to make life easier for her?

Much as it hurt her to admit it, life was so much easier without Kathleen. Maybe she just hadn't been up to the challenge of dealing with her daughter and her effect on her kids. Maybe if she had been a stronger person, she would have been able to handle it.

"Nonsense," her dad had said when she had mentioned it. "I've seen how you have handled those kids, raising them since Dale's death and now raising your grandkids. There's no one stronger than you. You have done right by your kids and your grandkids. Sometimes despite our best efforts our kids go their own way. Kathleen made choices and now she has to live with them. She doesn't have the right to drag anyone else down with her and that's what you would be doing if you pursued this line of thinking. It's not your fault Kathleen is in jail. She managed that on her own and one of the consequences is that she lost her kids. You didn't take them away from her. She lost them. I'll hear nothing more on this."

She had been surprised by her dad's vehemence. He was usually so soft spoken and slow to insert his opinion. Clearly she had hit a nerve. Still she appreciated the strength of his conviction. If only she could convince herself as well.

She threw the mail down on the table, sat down and opened the letter from Kathleen.

"What's up?" her dad had come into the kitchen for water.

"A letter from Kathleen."

"Oh, what does she have to say?"

She opened the letter and read it through before handing it to him. He laid it down after reading it, trying to digest its contents.

"So, she's going to be getting out," he said.

"Yes," Esther replied, not knowing what else to say. Kathleen wanted to see her boys.

"What are you going to do?"

"I don't know yet," Esther replied. What should she do? Her daughter is getting out of prison. She should be happy, shouldn't she? Instead she felt an impending dread. Like she didn't have enough to deal with – having no job and Joy's surgery coming up?

"We've got some time yet to think about it," she added, tucking the letter in her purse for another time. "First we've got to get Joy through her surgery, then I'll deal with this," she told herself.

Chapter 21

Esther read and re-read the letter. Kathleen was expecting to be released in a month. She wanted Esther to pick her up, was hoping to stay with her. Esther still didn't know what to do. She was her daughter, if only she had changed. What complicated the situation was that Josh had found out.

She hadn't been thinking when she had told him to get money out of her purse to pay for pizza. Josh had come back, letter in hand.

"What's this, grandma? Is this from mom?"

"Yes," she hadn't known what to tell him but now it had been decided. He already knew.

"Is she coming home? Are you picking her up?" Apparently Josh had read the letter in her purse. She had put it there because she had wanted to have easy access to it to read it over as she figured out what to do. If only she could read between the lines. Kathleen wasn't giving away anything. The letter had been short, newsy yet straight-forward. She hadn't included any clues as to how she was actually doing, whether she had changed her ways, learned her lessons while in jail, or had learned other lessons, whether she had picked up more bad habits from her time in jail.

"I don't know," Esther had said. Seemed she was saying that a lot lately. She didn't know much about anything these days.

"Is mom coming home?" Scott chimed in.

"Maybe," Esther said.

"According to this letter she's getting out in July," Josh said.

"I want to see her," Scott stated.

"That you will. That can be arraigned. Right now I've got a lot to figure out."

"What's there to figure out? She's our mom, she needs a home," Josh said.

"It's not as simple as that," her dad had intervened.

"Look, I'm not saying no. I just need to think about it."

"Well, think hard," Josh had said, "I'm not hungry." He went upstairs to his room.

Esther hadn't expected this. She wasn't sure what she had expected, just not this. Josh had always been her advocate, her support whenever something had come up involving his mom. Josh knew about the birthday and Christmas presents, knew who had actually bought them. She had thought he would have been on her side about this, not that she had a side yet. That's part of what bothered her. She didn't know what she was going to do.

She went upstairs and knocked on the bedroom Josh shared with his brother.

Josh grunted. She took that as the okay to come in.

"I'm sorry you found out the way you did. I was going to tell you, once I had figured a few things out."

"She is our mother."

"I know that. What do you think I should do?" Josh had been surprised at this question. He hadn't expected to be consulted. He paused. Scott had been too young to remember much about their mother. He still thought of her like the tooth fairy, granting wishes, delivering presents. Josh remembered more about her. They weren't always the best memories. He knew his grandmother had been the one who had always been there for him, taking care of him while his mother slipped away with her friends, promising to come back, coming back for a short while then disappearing again. Then when they would visit her in jail, she acted like she was so interested in what they were doing, only to start saying things about grandma that had confused him, demanding money from grandma, expecting grandma to do things she said she couldn't do. They would fight. He didn't know what to think at the time. It had actually been a relief when they no longer visited. But still she was their mother.

"I want to see her."

"That you will then. But we'll see about her staying here with us. There's hardly enough room for the four of us as it is."

"I could move into the basement. We could fix it up. Mom could have this room."

"And what about Scott?"

"He could share the bedroom with grandpa."

"Well, I'll think about it."

She sat and thought long and hard. Maybe she could fix the basement, not for Josh, but for Kathleen. It would give Kathleen more privacy, but then she also wouldn't be able to keep an eye on her as well from there. Would she need to keep an eye on her?

She finally decided she needed to talk to Kathleen in person before she would know what to do. She hated to make the long drive to the prison, hated to be gone for a full day when Joy and Dale needed her but at least they had Sara and she wouldn't be gone long.

"Your sister is getting out soon," she told Dale.

"Oh," Dale had so much on his mind these days. He was worried about Joy. She just wasn't herself and didn't seem to be snapping out of the fog she was in. She had experienced some mild depression with the other births but nothing like this. Neither of them had experienced anything like this. Cancer, it was devouring their life. He didn't want to think about his sister right now.

"She wants to move back in with me."

"What, you can't do that, not after all of the problems before."

"Maybe it will be different this time. She's older."

"Maybe it will be worse."

"I know that's a possibility. Anyway, I'm going to see her on Thursday before I make any decision. I'll be back late Thursday if you need me."

"That's okay, mom. You've already done so much for us. Don't worry about it. Sara's here to help. We'll be fine. You do what you have to do. Just be careful. I don't want to see you or those boys hurt."

"I will," Esther assured him but the one she needed to assure was herself.

Chapter 22

The three hour drive to the state prison gave Esther plenty of time to relive old memories. They were not ones she relished. She would have much rather have forgotten them. But here they were, popping up un-summoned into her brain where she had to deal with them. Memories of Kathleen as a child, how spunky she had been. Memories of her after Dale's death, how lost she had been, how one minute she seemed fine, the next she was crawling into her lap asking when daddy would come home. She had definitely been a daddy's girl.

Then those terrible teen years, staying out late, hanging out with the wrong crowd, sneaking out of the house after midnight and the drugs. Esther's efforts at tough love only seemed to push her farther away from her, farther down the path she had chosen till she moved out and moved in with friends when she had turned seventeen. She had finished high school. Esther didn't know how and didn't ask. She knew Kathleen had been haphazard in her attendance even when living at home despite Esther's best efforts. She had been smart enough to pass her classes doing a minimal amount of work.

"If you would put as much effort into doing your school work as you do avoiding it, you would graduate at the top of your class with a scholarship," Esther remembered telling her. Her words had fallen on deaf ears as Kathleen didn't listen. She was content to get by, finding new ways to avoid school work and work at home. It was a game, one Kathleen had thought she was winning.

Esther had taken away privileges one by one with no result. When she took away Kathleen's cell phone, she got another one, by what means, Esther didn't want to know. When she took away her driving privileges, Kathleen was un-fazed. She always had a back-up plan. She always found a way to get to where she wanted to go. It seemed she had "followers" who were only too happy to transport her wherever she wanted to go, both male and female.

Grounding her was ineffective as well. Esther needed to work. Who did she have to keep tabs on Kathleen? It wouldn't have been fair to ask Dale, Jr., to police his sister for her, making him the enforcer of curfews when she was at work. With no one to check on her, she would slip out. And even when Esther was home, Kathleen was adept at sneaking out.

When she first got into trouble with the law, Esther had hoped it would be a wake-up call for Kathleen or at least she would receive some assistance with how to handle her wayward daughter, but no. If anything, more restrictions were placed on Esther as the courts put punishments on Kathleen that Esther was supposed to enforce. She had thought some time in a juvenile home would be a welcome reprieve for her and provide Kathleen with the structure and supervision she appeared to need, but the judge kept giving her community service and placing her in after-school programs. Somehow, Esther, who was having a hard enough time keeping Kathleen in school, was supposed to make sure she attended both of these. At first the infractions had been minor ones, minor in possession, shoplifting some items, cigarettes, lighters, cosmetics. As the people she hung out with were caught for more serious crimes, Kathleen managed to get away with no charges.

While her moving out at seventeen had been something of a relief, Esther still remained responsible in the eyes of the law and was called into account for Kathleen's actions. Once she graduated Kathleen disappeared for a while, moving to a larger city with friends. She broke off all contact until she showed up four years later at twenty-two, hooked on drugs and pregnant with Josh. Esther had taken her in with the understanding that there would be no drugs as long as Kathleen was under her roof. Kathleen went through rehab and managed to stay clean until Josh's birth. Esther had thought that maybe now she would settle down and raise her son, only to have her return to her old habits little more than a month after Josh's birth, slipping out again at night and slipping away from her.

"I just have to get out, mom. Maybe you can stand it cooped up in a house with a baby, but I can't," she had told her. "I won't be late," she had insisted that first night, but that night had led to more nights and days. Esther had put up with it for Josh's sake, but after six months, Kathleen disappeared again, leaving behind only a note.

"I can't take it any more in this town. I've got to leave. I'll send for Josh when I'm settled."

That was all Esther heard from her until two years later when she showed up, pregnant once again. Again Esther took her in.

Kathleen was good with Josh during this time, watching him, spending time with him, freeing Esther from the need to put him in day care. Once again Esther hoped Kathleen had finally come around, had finally learned her lesson and was ready to raise her two children, only to have her hopes smashed.

This time Kathleen didn't even wait six months before leaving Esther with her two children. She did come back at times to visit and would call and talk to Josh. Each time she visited Josh would cling to her and beg her to stay. He would cry when she would go out with friends, leaving Esther to comfort him. It came as no surprise when Esther heard about her arrest. She hadn't known what Kathleen was involved in; just that she had money and no visible means of acquiring it. She had figured it was drugs, or boyfriend drug dealers. Either way, it wasn't good for Kathleen or her kids. There had been earlier arrests and some jail time, but this one was more serious.

Kathleen had wanted her to come to the trial so Esther had taken time off work, arranged child care for Josh and Scott and spent money she didn't have on a hotel during the trial. It had been short, over in just a few days. The evidence against Kathleen had been compelling. She had opted for a bench trial, not wanting to face a jury and hoping for a benevolent judge. Instead she received the maximum sentence. Esther sat in quiet pain as she watched the proceedings. This time, she thought, maybe this time, Kathleen would learn. She almost seemed different, subdued, no longer the cock-sure youth. Or was that too just a masquerade put on to fool her and the judge? If only she knew, Esther thought. If only Kathleen would get her life together, then all of this, all the pain would be worth it.

She had visited Kathleen after the verdict.

"Thank you for coming, mom. My lawyer said that if I had some family present showing support the judge might go easier on me. We've asked for an expedited sentence. The quicker I get sentenced, the quicker I can get this over with and the quicker I get sent to a more permanent place and get out of this jail. We are going to ask if I can be sent to a facility closer to home. You will visit me, won't you? And bring Josh and Scott?"

Esther made no promises but assured her she would do what she could.

When Kathleen was given the maximum sentence the next day she didn't flinch.

"I recognize that you say you are accepting responsibility for your role in this crime, however your past record tells me otherwise. You have a record of arrests with each one being more serious. That tells me that you haven't been given sufficient time to recognize the error of your ways and change," the judge had said before passing sentence.

Esther had wondered what Kathleen was thinking. Was she as resigned as she appeared? She saw her again briefly before leaving. She had been angry and hardly said a word. That was the angry Kathleen she had remembered from her teen years.

"Damn female judge. Has she no feelings for a mother of two young children?" she had complained.

At a loss for words, Esther had said good-bye. On the way home she decided to go through with the application to have maternal rights terminated and receive full custody, adopting Josh and Scott. She had been advised to do this repeatedly before, but had held off in hope that Kathleen would come around, that something would change. Faced with a possible twelve years it made no sense to delay any longer. Still part of her resisted. It seemed like a cruel slap to someone who was down, but maybe that was what Kathleen needed to finally get right. Even more important, maybe this was what the boys needed. They needed stability, someone they could count on to be there for them. That someone was her.

Through all those years, Dale Jr. had observed Kathleen and how her actions affected his mom. It seemed that he was the complete opposite to his sister, perhaps in reaction to her. Kathleen had never had time for church once she was old enough to resist Esther's efforts to get her there. When she went she made trouble for everyone, slouching and pouting, not participating. Esther had tried to get her to go to youth group with no luck. Dale, on the other hand, was active in the youth group at church, eventually taking a position of leadership along with Joy. He was as good as Kathleen was bad, which also worried Esther. It was too much to put on his young shoulder, this trying to make up for his sister's failings. Esther hadn't asked it of him. He had decided this all on his own it seemed.

There had been a year when Dale had shared an apartment with a friend, but the reality of cooking, cleaning, laundry, besides all of the additional expenses made home seem like a much better option. There he was able to focus more on work, spending the long hours he needed to get his business on firm footing, while helping his mom some with rent and groceries and sharing in the chores instead of being totally responsible. It had been a good arrangement for all parties until he was ready to begin his life with Joy.

He had still been living at home during both pregnancies, while he learned his trade and gained experience. He had thought about moving out but his mom needed him, especially once left to raise Josh and Scott. When his grandpa had moved in to help, he considered moving out, but then he was saving money to go towards starting his own business and buying a house someday. It wasn't until Joy had moved back that he moved out, into the house he had purchased with her at his side, in the hope of making it their home. By then the boys were in grade school and his grandfather was firmly entrenched in the house so they could get by without him. Still he had felt guilty moving out.

"Go on, get on with your life. You have put your life on hold for far too long. It's time you had a life of your own," Esther had said.

"Mom, you know that's not true. I haven't put my life on hold for you. If anything, it's been on hold while I got myself financially set and waited for Joy. If anything, you've been helping me get on my feet, giving me a place to live until I was ready for my own place."

"Either way, it's time for you to get out," Esther had said, both of them knowing how hard it was for her to say this. "Now go on," she told him as he moved out the last of his stuff.

"Oh, boy," Josh said, "can I have Uncle Dale's room?" As babies they had shared a room with their mom whenever she was around, and then with her when Kathleen wasn't around until they were old enough to be on their own in one room. When her dad had moved in she had fixed up the basement for Dale and moved her dad into Dale's old room.

"Nice try, Josh," Esther had said. Josh was all too eager to get away from Scott. "I can't have you so far away from me," she told him. "Maybe when you are older." The basement had gone back to storage.

Dale had been waiting for Esther when she came back from the trial and sentencing. He had also been among those advising her to get legal custody.

"Mom, there's no sense in waiting any longer. Even if Kathleen gets out early for good time, we are still looking at a minimum of eight years. Josh will be fourteen by then, Scott twelve. You owe it to them and to yourself to get this taken care of. And while you are at it, get your will up-dated and make me guardian of the boys should anything happen to you."

"Since when did you get so smart?"

"Since I've been taking these business classes so I'll know how to take care of the management end of my business. Besides, I got it from you. You've got a good head on your shoulders. How else would you have been able to do all that you have on your own? I've had a good teacher."

And so she had applied for and received legal custody of Kathleen's children. Kathleen had protested the loss of her maternal rights, tried to fight it, but with a twelve-year sentence, she had little grounds to stand on and little money for an attorney so it had gone through.

This had been another source of contention between mother and daughter. Esther had so hoped that Kathleen would have seen the necessity of this and gone along without any trouble but once again where Kathleen was concerned, her hopes had been dashed. What's worse is that she felt Kathleen tried to use the lawsuit against her when she brought Josh and Scott to visit, explaining why they were so difficult afterwards.

And now, here she was asking to come home. Esther wondered what good would come out of this.

Chapter 23

It had always been hard, visiting Kathleen in prison. She didn't like being frisked before being allowed in and then seeing Kathleen in prison garb, seeing the guards and the other inmates. It had not made for a pleasant experience in the past and was no pleasanter this time.

"Hi, mom," Kathleen said, reaching across the table to take her hands. She didn't know what to say. To say she looked good seemed a stretch. Who looks good in prison garb? To say it's good to see her was a bit much as well. She wasn't sure how glad she was to see her. She decided to let Kathleen take the lead.

"It's good to see you," Kathleen said. "How are Josh and Scott?"

"They're good, growing like weeds."

"Thank you for the pictures. At least they won't be complete strangers when I see them."

"So, you getting out soon?"

"Yes, if all goes well, next month. I could be home by mid-July. I will have to make arrangements with my probation officer but that shouldn't be any problem."

Again Esther didn't know what to say. It sounded like it was all settled as far as Kathleen was concerned.

"About that, about coming home . . ." she started.

"That is okay, isn't it, mom? I don't have anywhere else to go and I want to see the boys."

Esther paused before answering her, "How long are you thinking of staying?" she asked cautiously.

"I'm not planning on staying with you permanently but at least until I get on my feet, get a job and all. That's okay with you, isn't it?"

"Well, that's just it. I don't know yet. What are you planning on doing?"

"First I just want to reconnect with my boys."

"So you're planning on moving back to town. What about your friends in Chicago? I thought you hated it at home."

"I thought I did too. It's amazing what eight years in prison can do to a person. Look, mom, I know I haven't been the best daughter to you or mother to my boys, but I'd like to try to make it up to you if you give me a chance."

"How do I know this time will be different?"

"Because I'm different. I'm older, wiser."

"And what will you do? What work?"

"I'll take any job I can get. I'll work at MacDonald's if that's all that's available. I've been able to take some computer classes while here. I'm quite good at web design and trouble shooting. I thought I might be able to get a job doing that, or I thought maybe I could work for Dale for a while at his business. I could set up a website for him. But if not, I'll find something. I'm willing to do whatever it takes to make things work, to make it right with you and Dale and my boys. What do you say, mom?"

"I don't know. I have to talk it over with Dale and with your grandpa. You know he's living with us now."

"Yes, you told me that. How is he?"

"He's good, doing good, getting older but then aren't we all?"

"I know that. Try turning thirty-five in prison. I've wasted way too many years," she paused, waiting for a response.

"Well, as I said. I'll think about it, talk it over with the boys and grandpa and let you know."

"That would be good, mom, no pressure, although I do need to know before I leave."

"I'll let you know well before then." They chit-chatted for a while after that along with sitting through some awkward silences as Esther waited for the end to visiting time. She was relieved to have a guard tell her it was time to go.

"Bye, mom, it was good to see you," Kathleen said as she was escorted out of the room.

"I'll let you know," Esther responded.

Chapter 24

Much as Dale wanted to know how his mom's visit with his sister had gone, Dale also didn't want to know. Good news can wait. And bad news? Well, bad news hung around like dirty, wet laundry leaving a lingering musty smell. There was no way there could be good news with anything that involved Kathleen, so no rush to hear it. He had enough trouble on his mind. There was no room for any more.

Sara had taken the two older children to the park and then for ice cream, giving Joy and him some much-needed time alone. They had had so little time to themselves since the baby had been born. Much as he loved his mom and Joy's sister, and much as he appreciated their help, he looked forward to it just being Joy and him and their children, to getting back to some sense of normalcy. He knew that wouldn't be happening any time soon, not with surgery and the regimen of radiation they had ahead of them. Still, in the distance, he saw that glimmering hope of a cancer-free wife and a family routine where running out of toilet paper was the biggest crisis they encountered. Would they ever have that life, he wondered.

He would be happy to have his wife back. Joy had always been a fighter; not only that, her name had fit her. Easy-going and full of fun, she had been a joy to live with. Even when first confronted with cancer, she had maintained her calm spirit and ability to appreciate life's little wonders. All that had disappeared since coming home from the hospital after Grace's birth. She had checked over her new baby in wonder at what her body had produced despite the battle raging inside of her, but then after assuring herself that baby Grace was okay, she had slipped into a slump.

Surgery was scheduled for next week. They had decided on a double mastectomy in order to keep her from having to go through this again. The doctor had put her on medication to dry up her milk in preparation for the surgery. Dale had expected more of a fight over this but Joy seemed to have lost her will to fight. She would need it before going into surgery. Dale didn't know what to do, or what to say to this stranger who had come to inhabit his wife's body.

Joy put baby Grace down for the night, the baby content from the bottle of breast milk Joy had managed to pump before beginning to take the medicine. Already her breasts were feeling less full. She had nursed her baby one last time with what little remained, then switched to the bottle.

"There Gracie, I've done all I can, now time for you to step up. You'll have to learn how to live on formula, not mommy's milk."

Dale stood at the door to the nursery, watching Joy put Grace down.

"Ready for something to eat?" he asked. Sara and the kids had eaten before going to the park. He had waited in order to sit down with Joy.

Joy nodded, turned on the baby monitor and followed Dale downstairs.

"We can eat out on the porch," he suggested. It was a balmy summer evening as the cool of early June gave way to late June.

"That would be nice." Joy allowed herself to be waited on, sitting down at the table on the porch and waiting for Dale to bring her a plate of food. Pork chops, au gratin potatoes and broccoli. Esther had prepared it before going home, leaving their portion on the stove, ready to be reheated in the microwave. It looked unappetizing to her even though it had once been a favorite. Everything looked and smelled unappetizing lately, and she wasn't even on chemo.

Joy picked at her meal then pushed it back.

"Come on, Joy, you've got to eat. You've got to build up your strength before the surgery. If your white blood cell count isn't where it needs to be, the doctor will postpone the surgery."

"And that would be bad because . . .?" Joy asked.

"We can't put this off forever, not if we are going to beat this thing."

"The thing is cancer. It has a name."

"Okay, not if we are going to beat this cancer." Dale looked over at Joy. She seemed devoid of all emotion, not sad, not angry, nothing. "Joy, talk to me. Tell me what's wrong. We've always managed before as long as we worked together. We are in this together. Don't shut me out."

"No, we aren't in this together. I'm the one who has cancer."

"No, we have cancer, our family has cancer. You may be the one dealing with the physical aspects but all of us are affected."

"But you aren't the one about to become deformed. You're not losing an important part of your anatomy."

"I feel like I'm losing you. You are more important to me than my body, than your body or your breasts. You, the girl I married. Only you know me like you do. Only you share so many parts of my life. I don't know what I would do without you. It feels like I have already lost you. We are in this together, aren't we?"

"I don't know, Dale. I just don't know anything anymore. I'm so tired. I'm tired of everything and yet when I sleep I get no rest. I wake up just as tired as when I went to bed. Do you know what I mean?"

"I know. I've felt you tossing and turning at night."

"Have I been keeping you awake? I didn't mean to."

"Don't worry about it. This is part of sharing our lives, sharing our bed."

"I can't have you not sleeping too."

"What we can't have is you tossing and turning alone, feeling alone in this."

"But I am alone. Don't you see, I am alone. We all face death alone. We come into this world alone and we go out alone."

"No, we come into this world into loving welcoming arms, just like Grace did, into our parents' embrace. And we don't go out alone, we go into our Father's embrace. When it is time and if that happens, I will be there with you to the very end. But that isn't going to happen, not any time soon. That will be after our sixtieth wedding anniversary and you will be surrounded by grown children and grandchildren, maybe even great grandchildren. We've got a lot of living to do between then and now. We just have to get through these next few months."

"Dale, I'm so afraid." Joy began to cry.

"It's okay, Joy. It's okay to be afraid when confronted by death. It's okay to cry. What isn't okay is for you to shut me out. What isn't okay is for you to give up. I need you to fight for your life. The kids need you to fight for your life."

Joy allowed the tears she had been holding back to flow freely. Dale held her while she cried, awkwardly rubbing her back, unsure whether to say anything more, whether to try to lighten the mood with a joke or to cry himself. Instead he waited for Joy to be done, to have spent all her tears till her eyes were as dry as her breasts would soon be.

"I'm sorry," Joy said as she raised her head from Dale's shoulder. "I'm afraid I have been very selfish. I haven't been thinking about you or the kids. I've just been wallowing in self-pity. I just needed to do this for a while. I needed to wallow for awhile, but now I see it's time to start fighting again, to re-engage in life. I had mentally checked out, but I will be better," she assured him.

"It's okay to wallow now and then. It's okay to think about yourself, just don't give in or give up. You're a fighter. I need you to be a fighter. Can you do that for me?"

"I'll try."

"You can start by eating your dinner. I'll heat it up for you," Dale said taking both plates back into the kitchen.

"Thank you. It almost sounds good," Joy said with a slight smile.

"And for dessert, ice cream," Dale said as he returned.

"With chocolate?"

"With chocolate."

The change wasn't overnight but Dale could tell something had shifted inside Joy. When he talked with his pastor about it he had referred Dale to the Psalms of Lament.

"Sometimes the people with the deepest faith also suffer the deepest grief, but they make it through. They go down to the depths and they come back up again. They aren't afraid of deep feelings. Read the Psalms. The writers were not afraid of deep feelings. Neither should we be. Joy will pull through this," he had assured him.

Dale wasn't as sure. Sometimes people go down to the depths and they don't make it out. Still, who was he to question his pastor? To question God? And yet the writers of the Psalms seemed to do just that, he found when he picked the Bible up. He didn't get it.

Something else his pastor had said, that joy is suffering that has been worked through. He hoped so. He so hoped that joy would return to his life, to the life he shared with his wife. He had written this down on a scrap of paper and put it in his briefcase along with work-related papers he carried with him. If only Joy can work through this, he thought.

"What are you doing?" Joy asked when he didn't come to bed.

"I'm reading the Psalms. You go on back to bed. I'll be there shortly."

Chapter 25

"So, how did it go? Is mom coming home?" Josh asked. Her dad, Josh and Scott had been waiting for her when she got back.

"Whoa, give your grandma a break. Give her a chance to take a breath, have something to eat."

"Thank you, dad," Esther said as she sat down and accepted the glass of lemonade he had poured.

Esther didn't know what to say. She knew Josh would be expecting an answer. She had thought about it the whole drive home. What to do? Kathleen seemed better, but she had been deceived before. Still she was her daughter. She couldn't deny that. Finally she had turned on the radio and tried to drown out her thoughts with music.

"Josh and Scott, would you give your great grandpa and me some time?"

"Why? You are going to talk about my mom. I have a right to hear."

"Because I said so. You know I don't play this card too often. I'm playing it now. We'll talk later."

"Come on, Scott, we're not wanted here," Josh said as he left the room. Esther ignored his comment. She could tell he was not happy, yet he had obeyed. So different from his mother, she thought. Kathleen never obeyed; she fought her with every breath. Would that change if she were living with them, would Josh become more like her?

"I don't know, dad, she seems to be better but I can't tell. I'm thinking I've got to give her this chance."

"Do you? How many times do you have to give someone a second chance?"

"Seventy times seven, seems that's what Jesus said."

"That was forgiveness. Just because you forgive someone doesn't mean you have to give them a second chance to mess up. Sometimes the most loving thing is to forgive and to set boundaries."

"I know, dad. I know all about tough love and setting boundaries. Guess who I learned it from."

"Kathleen."

"Yes, Kathleen. She forced me to learn, forced me to parent in a way I never would have expected to have to parent, forced me to be tough and set limits on what I could accept. It wasn't an easy lesson but I learned it."

"So what is different now?"

"So much time has passed."

"Have you forgotten?"

"No, but maybe she deserves another chance. People do change, maybe she has. Getting older, life experience can change us."

"Or set us more stubbornly in our ways."

"I know that can happen." Esther had lived long enough to have seen both happen.

"What does your heart tell you?"

Esther paused, took a sip of lemonade before answering, "To give her another chance."

"Then I guess that's what we have to do. We'll give her a chance, but we'll do so with caution."

"Yes, this isn't a green light. It's a yellow light, proceed with caution."

Chapter 26

Sara and Esther swept Joy away for a "Bye-bye boobies" party. Sara had made arrangements with Dale for him to take care of all three kids for the night. Esther had abandoned her dad and the boys for the night.

"Go out for pizza," she told them. "This is a girls' only party."

They decorated the lounge area at the dance studio with balloons and fake boobs.

"You've got a real talent for this," Esther had told Sara as Sara came up with the finishing touches for the party.

"You think it will get me a job? Party planner, specializing in boobies."

"Definitely," Esther laughed. There was "bib" lettuce, chicken breasts in a milk sauce and for dessert chocolate cupcakes with white cream cheese frosting shaped like breasts with red hots serving as nipples. For drinks they had pina coladas and they were going to finish off the evening with foaming hot lattes.

After dinner they would play pin the breast on the super model and then would use Scot's toy laser guns to play zap the boob, hunting down and eradicating cancer cells. They had also brought a Pac Man game so they could play that Pac Man was eating cancer cells.

They had considered inviting some of Joy's friends but had decided against it just in case Joy wasn't up for a party. The way she had been recently they weren't sure what kind of reception they would get so they thought it best to keep it small. They had been having so much fun planning for this party. The question was, would Joy have as much fun?

They had gone to Joy's home and kidnapped her.

"You're coming with us, no questions asked," Sara had insisted so that Joy could not say no. They were both relieved when Joy laughed at the decorations.

"Surprise! This is your farewell to boobies party. No one should have to say goodbye to their breasts without giving them an appropriate farewell," Esther said while Sara draped Joy in gauzy light fabric designed to make her feel like a princess. Sara placed a crown on her turbaned head and gave her a toy light saber as a scepter. "You are Princess Joy. Your scepter is for commanding your loyal subjects and for zapping errant cancer cells."

Dinner went off without a hitch. It was good to see Joy laugh at the food and games. As they were preparing for another round of pin the boob on the supermodel they heard a knock.

"Who's that?" Esther wondered out loud. "No one knows we are here."

She answered the door and was surprised by Joy's mom.

"I heard there was a party here," she said with a hesitant smile. "I hope it's all right that I came."

"Of course you're welcome, Mary, come on in," Esther said as she held the door open for her.

"Mom," Sara and Joy both said as she came in.

"I hope I'm not intruding. Dale had told me you would be here. He had said something about a 'boob' party."

Her daughters laughed at hearing their mother use a term so completely not part of her vocabulary. "Of course you're welcome, mom. We're sorry we didn't tell you. We weren't sure whether you would be comfortable at a … such a party," Sara said, jumping to give her mom the seat next to Joy.

"We also weren't sure Joy would be up for a party so we wanted to keep it small," Esther added.

"That's fine, no need to explain. I didn't know what one would bring to a 'booby' party, but I made some of my divinity." Mary opened the box she had been carrying and showed rows of white divinity shaped like little breasts.

"Mom, that's great. They're perfect," Sara said.

"Nothing's too good for my perfect daughter," she said giving Joy a kiss, tearing up as she did so.

"Can I get you anything?" Esther asked. "Coffee?"

"Decaf would be great," Mary responded as Esther went to the kitchen and came back with dessert and coffee.

"The coffee will go great with your divinity, mom," Sara said. There was a lull in the conversation as each ate their desserts. Mary broke the silence.

"I hear your daughter is coming home soon, Esther." Joy looked up from her dessert and exchanged looks with Esther. Her mom sure knew how to bring a party down, she thought. Sara saw the look pass between Joy and Esther. She didn't know what was going on.

"Yes, she is," Esther stated.

"You must be happy, finally to have her home again."

"Yes, well, we'll see." Dale and Esther hadn't told Joy yet. They were going to wait until after the surgery, didn't want to have her upset over anything else over which she had no control. Joy remembered far too well what it had been like for Dale during high school, all the problems Kathleen had caused not just for her mom, but for Dale as well. She didn't want to think about it just then. We'll talk later; Esther's look had told her. Okay, Joy's eyes had responded.

Sara watched the silent interchange then jumped up and came back with presents.

"Time for presents!" she said.

"Presents? Isn't this party enough?" Joy said. "Besides, what do you give at a 'booby' party?"

Sara set a box wrapped in creamy white paper and tied with a pink ribbon in front of her. "See for yourself," she said.

Joy gasped and teared up as she pulled out the series of four framed sketches, each of her in different stages of pregnancy, dressed in her leotard and wrap around.

"Sara, they're perfect."

"I wanted you to have something to remind you of how you looked before your surgery. Here I have one more." Sara handed her a large, flat, wrapped object.

"Oh, Sara, when did you find time to do this?" Joy cried as she opened an oil painting of her in her ballet clothes with rounded belly and turbaned head, one toe pointing behind her and her arms raised in praise, balancing on a wire high above the clouds while the sun shone on her face. Around her were clouds and angels ready to catch her if she should fall. "It's beautiful."

"It's to remind you to keep your balance, no matter what life may give you. It's a reminder to keep on dancing no matter what. And it's a reminder that you are not alone. You've got angels watching over you, and you've got us," Sara said, reaching for Joy's hand and sitting down beside her.

"That you have," Esther assured her.

"Thank you all. This has been the perfect send off. I don't know how to thank you," Joy said as she continued to look at her picture.

"By getting through this," Sara said as she wrapped her arm around Joy's waist.

"That I will."

Joy's mother just cried. "I'm so sorry. I didn't come here to drag down the party," she said through her tears. "It's just you, my beautiful daughters, both of you. You are so strong and I'm so proud." With that she hugged both of them while Esther looked on.

"Esther, come join us. You're part of the family too," Mary invited Esther over and hugged her. "I'm so glad my Joy has your son, Dale, to help her through this. And I'm so glad she has you, too. Now who wants another titty?" she said, offering the plate of divinity as they laughed.

Chapter 27

"I hear Kathleen is coming back," Joy said to Dale while waiting for the anesthesia to take effect.

"Oh," Dale said, unsure what to say. Was he in trouble for not telling her, he wondered. "Who told you?"

"My mom, don't worry," she said as she faded out. "We can talk about it later."

Kathleen coming back hadn't been good news but it was out of his hands. His mom wanted to give her another chance. That was her choice. It didn't have to be his choice. He didn't know what he would do yet. He had too much to worry about with Joy and the kids to let Kathleen into that precious circle of concern. Yet here she was, clogging his brain when he needed to be focused on Joy and her surgery. Still it gave him a break from his worries about Joy. It was a needed diversion, one he didn't want but maybe needed.

He, too, had memories where Kathleen was concerned, mostly negative ones. He didn't want her messing up the life he had so carefully established for himself and his family. She had written him, hoping to make amends but even more, hoping for a job. Why should he give her a job when there are so many others who needed jobs, others without a prison record, others with more, better experience and a clean work history?

"Because she's your sister," Joy had said when they finally had time to discuss Kathleen's pending homecoming.

"All the more reason not to hire her. There's always problems when you mix family and business. There's less accountability because they think they can get away with behavior you wouldn't tolerate from anyone else simply because they're a relative."

"Or there might be more accountability because it is family and they want to do right by family."

"Yes, but it could go either way. Experience tells me which way it will be for Kathleen."

"I'm not telling you what to do, but if your mom is willing to give Kathleen a chance, maybe we should to."

"That doesn't mean we have to give her a job."

"Enough said," Joy ended the discussion. "Let's talk about more pleasant subjects. How are the kids?"

The surgery had gone well. While not entirely back to her old self, still Joy was better than she had been. She even managed to joke with Dale about her loss.

"And to think, it was my breasts that kept me from going further in ballet. Now I'm the flat-chested image of the perfect ballerina, only I'm too old to perform. Now I'll have to learn how to dance all over again. I'll have to adjust to my new form."

"You're not too old, and you've always been perfect to me, always will be," Dale replied.

Joy had brought one of Sara's sketches with her and placed it into Dale's safe-keeping during the surgery. She would have brought the oil painting if it hadn't been so bulky. As it was, she carried the image in her brain. She imagined herself in the clouds, watched over by angels. The image gave her a sense of peace that carried her through the surgery. She had placed the picture in her bedroom where she would be able to look at it during recovery once she got home. She had set the sketch she had brought with her in her hospital room. It both cheered her and saddened her as she saw the person she had once been. She clung to it as a reminder of her sister's love.

Everyone who came into the room commented on the sketch.

"That's a remarkable likeness," her pastor had commented when he came to visit Joy and Dale in the hospital. "Who drew it?"

"Sara."

"Talent runs in your family."

"Yes, it does. She drew it as a before picture," Joy stated with a calmness her eyes didn't share.

"And how are you after this? What does the after picture look like?"

"I'm good, we're good," she said holding Dale's hand.

"Your eyes tell me something else," the minister quietly noted.

The tears that lurked in the corners swelled her eyes and spilled over as her voice cracked. "No, really, we are doing good," she assured him.

He reached over and took both of their hands. "I see your tears. It's okay. You don't have to be strong for me. You need that for your children. For now, it's okay to cry," he said as he prayed for both of them.

"Thank you," Dale said as Pastor Joe prepared to leave. "Let me walk you out," he added. "I'll see you first thing tomorrow," he said as he leaned over and gave Joy a kiss.

"Kiss the kids for me," Joy told him as he accompanied the minister out the door.

Joy was still wiping the tears from her eyes when her nurse came in.

"What a beautiful sketch. Is it you?" she asked.

"Yes, my sister did it." Joy welcomed the chance to talk about something besides herself and her surgery.

"It's a wonderful likeness. Is she local?"

"Yes, as a matter of fact she's staying with my kids right now. Why?"

"I would love to have some sketches of my kids. Do you think she would do that?"

"I can ask," Joy told her. "Or . . ." Joy paused as she wrote Sara's phone number on a napkin, "here's her phone number if you want to call her." She handed her the napkin.

"Maybe I will," she said, "Thank you. If you need anything just push the call button," she said as she turned off the lights.

Then it was just Joy alone with her memories of the woman she used to be.

Chapter 28

Sara still didn't have any job prospects. She wasn't overly concerned. After sending out hundreds of resumes with no luck, she had decided to give herself a reprieve from the job hunting sentence while helping Joy out. She had applied for multiple jobs but none had excited her.

"You don't need excitement," her dad had said. "You just need a job. Something to pay the bills."

She understood where he was coming from but still hoped for something more, something that involved her creative side.

Joy was escorted out of the hospital in a wheelchair, Sara's picture proudly displayed in her lap as if proclaiming to the world: I can overcome this.

"You know, there may be a market for your sketches," she told Sara when she arrived home.

"What are you talking about?"

"Your picture drew a lot of attention in the hospital. One person asked if you would consider sketching her children. I gave her your phone number. You really need a business card."

"Really," Sara said. She had considered trying something like this, but had dismissed it as too impractical. She needed a "real" job; her drawing would be a side line. Still, since she didn't have that real job yet, what would it hurt to give this a try?

"You could call it Sara's Studio of Design. I could give you space at the dance studio," Joy had suggested.

The idea intrigued her. It definitely was worth considering. Larry had already suggested as much. He was ready to construct a website for her. She wasn't sure what was holding her back. Maybe fear that no one would be interested in her artwork, fear of failing, of falling. Yet if Joy could keep balance going through her struggle with cancer, certainly she could give this a try, take a chance and not let fear hold her back.

"What's the worst that could happen?" Larry asked that night when they skyped.

"I could invest money I don't have and lose all of it. I could be a failure. Maybe no one will be willing to pay for my artwork."

"We can set it up for a minimal up-front cost. I'll take my payment for constructing your website out in trade," he said. Sara laughed.

"You won't be out too much money," Larry continued. "You can still look for other jobs while you do this but as long as you are not working, you might as well give this a try."

"And if I fail?"

"There is no failure. There are just bumps in the road of life. If you learn from your mistakes then it's not a failure."

Maybe Larry was right, Sara thought, not that she would admit it to him. They had maintained contact after graduation even though living in different cities. Larry, with his tech skills, was much more employable than she was. He already had a good paying job in Detroit, a job that required more than full-time hours. He didn't have a lot of free time for dating but she was okay with that for now. She wasn't sure how much time she wanted to devote to dating right now. It seemed that Joy's cancer had flowed over, infecting all who loved her. It was a near full-time job to support her through this, watching the kids, though Sara would never say this to Joy. She was happy to put her own life on hold for a while to help her big sister. It wasn't a burden. It was a joy. It was Joy!

Larry had offered to help her financially with the start-up costs for a business. "Don't look at it as a hand-out but as an investment. I'm investing in a promising new artist." Sara had refused his offer but it was nice to know that was a possibility.

"You've still got student loans to worry about repaying, as I do too. I can't ask you to do this," Sara told him.

"You're not asking. I'm offering. Think about it."

Sara was pleasantly surprised when the nurse Joy had told her about called. She met with her and agreed to produce a sketch of each of her three children. They negotiated a price and arranged for a time for Sara to meet her children and observe them at play in order to get a sense of their spirit. The price was not even close to paying for her time but it was a start. As she built her business, eventually she would be able to charge more. She didn't want to discourage potential customers by charging too much but needed to feel she was making enough to make it worth her time and effort.

The nurse had given Sara pictures of her children to work from. Someone else might have taken that and run with it but a picture didn't capture the essence of the individual the way actually watching them did. Sara wanted a sense of the person she was drawing. After that she drew several rough drafts in her sketch book before deciding on the ones she wanted to fine tune.

She showed her sketch book to the nurse and asked her which ones she liked best.

"You know, you could make money doing drawings at kid's parties," she had suggested. "You just do quick sketches. I know other mothers who might be interested. I can pass on your card. Do you have a flier or any other information?"

"Not yet, but I will."

Her first check for her artwork, Sara thought as she accepted payment for the completed pictures. This called for a celebration, she thought. The woman had been so impressed that she had given her more than the agreed upon amount.

She texted Larry to let him know and took a picture of herself holding the check and sent that to him as well.

"Congratulations!" he texted back. "You are on your way!"

She hurried back to Joy's, eager to share her good news. Joy was sleeping, weak from her latest bout with radiation. She would have to wait to tell her. Sara called Esther to see if she wanted to celebrate with her but Esther was busy preparing for Kathleen's eminent return. Sara had lost touch with most of her high school friends. She called Anne then Jeff to let them know her good news but after that she was left to herself. Feeling let down she sat on her bed in Joy and Dale's home. She heard the familiar chirp alerting her that a text message had been received.

"Turn on your computer," the text instructed. Sara turned it on.

"Go to www.sarastyles.com," the next text read.

Sara entered the web address and was amazed at what appeared. There was her face on a web page with Sara's Styles across the top. Featured on the left was the oil painting she had done of Joy. Designs, sketches, charcoal drawing, and oil paintings, were all listed. "Let Sara design the perfect logo for your business or the right art for your home or office," it stated. It included a contact page and a page of her work to click on. When she clicked she saw other examples of her artwork from her portfolio.

"What do you think?" Larry asked when she picked up the phone for his call.

"I love it."

"I was going to wait and give it to you for your birthday but I couldn't wait. I thought you needed something to commemorate your special day."

"It's wonderful, Larry."

"It's not done yet. I tried to integrate everything we had talked about. You still need to add your logo, once you design one. I also can add a page for a blog if you decide to do that."

"What would I include in a blog?"

"You could write about your life as an artist, the struggles of starting your own business or just write about your life. It's entirely up to you. It helps to add interest to your website so there is something more for those who click on the site to read. It's good to keep adding information, switching things up a bit to keep people interested. Nothing worse than a boring website that never changes."

"Thank you so much."

"You can thank me properly this weekend. We have to celebrate. Can you get away? Come to Detroit for a night out?"

"I don't know, Joy is still so weak and Esther is preoccupied with her daughter. I don't know that I can get away right now."

"Well, I could come to you. They certainly wouldn't object to a single night out."

They finally decided to meet half-way at a restaurant Larry had heard about off of I-94. That way they would both be able to get home to their own beds, for now.

A promising career, a website and a date for Saturday night, Sara congratulated herself. It just doesn't get better than this, she thought with a smile.

Chapter 29

Esther wasn't looking forward to Kathleen's return. Josh and Scott had been excited at first but as the reality drew closer they seemed a little unsure.

"Will mom remember me? I don't remember her," Scott had asked.

"Oh, yes, your mother remembers you. Can a mother forget her child?" Esther said. Josh had remained silent. Much as he had wanted to see his mother at first, his memories of her weren't always pleasant. He had mixed feelings.

Esther had been prepared to pick Kathleen up but had been relieved when Kathleen informed her that she would take the bus. "That way if there is any change in my release date you won't be inconvenienced," Kathleen told her. Esther thought that was a good sign. Kathleen was actually thinking about her and not wanting to inconvenience her.

Kathleen, for her part, welcomed the bus trip. After eight years locked up, she relished the freedom and had wanted a chance to sort out her feelings before being plunged back into her family. She wasn't sure about this, yet she didn't know where else to go, had no place to go.

Home is the place that when you go there, they have to let you in. Who had said that? She couldn't remember but liked the quote. She had had an abundance of time on her hands for reading. She had never much cared about reading in her youth but had found it to be a necessary escape from the boredom of prison life. Where others got into fights or idled away the time creating trouble, she had read voraciously. First legal books in search of an early out. She had become a jail house lawyer, advising other inmates in exchange for cigarettes and other favors. She didn't smoke the cigarettes but found them to be helpful as currency for purchasing other items she wanted. Then she had moved on to other books as she worked her way through the shelves of the prison library. At first it had just been a way to fill the long hours, but over time she began to relish the opportunity to read.

118

Home, home is wherever I hang my hat, she told herself. Her cell had been her home for so long. Now that was gone she felt rootless and unsettled, unsure about where she would land. Still she had wanted to see her kids so her mom's home seemed the best place to go, recoup and figure out what to do next. You would have thought that after all of the time on her hands in prison she would have had plenty of time to figure that out. But jailhouse dreams seldom materialized on the outside; she was smart enough to recognize that. She had made some plans but not too far in advance and even these she held lightly, unsure what life would bring her. One thing she was sure about, she told herself, she would not spend any more time behind bars. Once out she would be smarter: she wouldn't be caught.

Kathleen didn't have a phone to call Esther to pick her up at the bus station so she decided to take a cab, paying from the small stash of cash she had been able to make while in jail. It wasn't much but there would be more, Kathleen assured herself as she counted out some bills for the cabby.

She stood at the curb, her possessions in a backpack slung from her shoulder, unsure about whether to go in or run in the opposite direction.

Nowhere to go but forward, Kathleen told herself and approached the door.

"Hi grandpa," Kathleen said when he opened the door. She hugged him with a false sense of bravado then walked through the door. "The place hasn't changed much," she said as she looked around. "Mom told me you had moved into my old room. Where do I stay?"

"Why didn't you call for a ride?" Esther asked, walking in from the kitchen.

"No phone, besides I didn't want to bother you."

"You'll be in the basement, in Dale's old room. I fixed it up for you." She gave her daughter a hesitant hug. "Do you want to take your bags down now?"

"Just this backpack. I'm travelling light," Kathleen responded. "I would like to check it out."

Josh and Scott came out of the living room, awkwardly standing in the doorway.

"You come here," Kathleen said. "Josh, Scott, you're both so big. I hardly recognize you. The pictures your grandmother sent me didn't capture how big you've grown."

"Hi mom," Josh extended his hand for her to shake.

"Come here, give your mom a hug," Kathleen said, pulling him into her arms then hugging Scott.

"Josh, why don't you take your mom downstairs? I'll finish dinner. Scott, you can set the table. We'll be eating in a half an hour," Esther issued instructions.

Josh showed his mom the space they had set up for her in the basement. It was nothing fancy, just a bed, dresser and TV, but at least it was cool and dry. A fan had been placed in a corner and turned on to welcome her.

"It isn't much. I told mom I would sleep down here but then you would have had to share with Scott or Scott would have had to move in with great grandpa. Better this way, I guess."

"That's okay, Josh. I'll get along just fine." Josh left her to unpack her few belongings. Kathleen looked about the room. She didn't know what she had expected. She knew that there were only three bedrooms and four people already living here. Still, this was little better than her cell in prison, although there she had a toilet. At least there was a window even if it was just a small rectangular slot at the top of the room. It would do for now, she told herself. She didn't know how long she would stay.

Dinner was good despite a certain awkwardness. It was good to taste her mom's barbecue chicken and potato salad again. She had forgotten just how good it was.

"I would have made a pie but it's so hot. I didn't want to turn on the oven."

"That's okay, mom. It was great. Thanks for dinner. So boys, how have you been? Fill me in. Josh, you are so handsome, do you have a girlfriend yet? And Scott, what about you? It's so good to see you." Kathleen was trying to work her magic on the boys. "How about we get some ice cream?" she suggested.

"Sure," Scott agreed. Josh was reluctant.

"Go ahead, Josh. I can take care of the dishes," Esther had insisted.

"There's still the Tasty-Treat within walking distance, isn't there?" Kathleen asked.

"It's still there, you go on." When they came back Esther sat on the porch with her daughter.

"So, what are your plans?"

"Don't know yet. First I have to check in with my new probation officer. And I guess I better get a phone. Can't do anything without a phone these days. Then I'll start job hunting. How are Dale and Joy?"

"They're okay, as good as can be expected in light of everything."

"Maybe I'll stop by to see them tomorrow," Kathleen said then excused herself. "It's been a long day," she said as she retreated to the basement. "Oh, and I need to get a driver's license. Can you drive me tomorrow?"

Chapter 30

Kathleen kept busy re-establishing herself, applying for a driver's license, getting a cell phone, meeting with her probation office and looking for work. She also kept Esther busy driving her places until she got her license. Then it was a matter of borrowing a car to get around.

"Come on, grandpa, you aren't using your car," she said, coaxing a car out of her grandfather. He didn't drive a lot; still he had been reluctant to give up his "baby." He had a coffee klatch at a local restaurant every morning. It was his way of staying in touch with old friends and finding out all the news. After that his car was usually available. "It's either that or drive me places," Kathleen had said.

"But don't get used to it," he had said as he handed over his keys. Isn't that what grandfathers are supposed to do--supply cars to grandchildren, he thought, once they were no longer able to drive themselves. He had seen a number of his friends give up their driving privileges at the insistence of their kids. He wasn't there yet and resisted any attempt to bump him off the road before his time. He was concerned that this was a veiled attempt to gradually get him out of the driver's seat and so resisted. He insisted Kathleen return his keys the minute she got back home each day.

Armed with a car and a cell phone, Kathleen summed up the courage to visit her brother at work.

"Yo, little brother," she said with a smile.

"Kathleen, I heard you were back," he didn't return her smile. "What's up?"

"Can't a sister visit her brother without wanting something?"

"Cut the crap, Kathleen, what do you want?"

"Okay, Dale, you know what I want. I need a job. Can't you use someone in your office, someone knowledgeable about computers?"

"I have an administrative assistant and IT people on contract whenever there is a computer problem."

"Well, then, do you know of anyone who's hiring?"

"No, I'm sorry, Kathleen. It's a tough job market right now. You should know that. Mom's been looking for a job for the past nine months. Joy's sister is job hunting. There's just not a lot out there."

"Especially if you have a record, which is why I had hoped you could help me, maybe you could pull some strings, call in some favors?"

"I'll keep a look-out for openings, but don't count on it."

"Dale, you know I need to get some work experience if I'm ever to be hired. What if I work in your office for free, just to get some hours to my credit?"

"I don't know if that is a good idea," Dale hesitated.

"Just give me a chance, Dale. If my own brother won't give me a chance, who will?" Kathleen insisted.

"Let me think about it."

"What's there to think about, free office help? It's a no-brainer, little brother," Kathleen said, poking him on the shoulder the way she used to when they were kids.

"All right, just on a trial basis, just a few hours a day," Dale agreed.

"That's great. The first thing I need to know is where the coffee pot is and do I get a company car and credit card."

"Wait just a minute."

"Just kidding, little brother, just kidding," Kathleen said with a smile. "When do I start?"

"Come in tomorrow afternoon and I'll get you set up."

"Don't worry, you won't regret this," Kathleen said as she left.

Dale doubted that. His stomach churned as he watched her leave. "I already do," he said to himself.

"That's good," Joy had affirmed his decision when he told her that night.

"You really think so, because I think it's a mistake."

"Yes, I do. If Kathleen's ever to rebuild a life someone has to give her a break."

"Then why does it feel so wrong?"

"It will be fine. Just give her a chance," Joy reassured him.

Chapter 31

Kathleen set about making herself indispensable. Dale's current office staff of one took none too kindly to her presence.

"Do I need to be worried about my job?" she asked Dale.

"No, not at all, Joyce. You know we couldn't get along without you."

"Good, you remember that because I just may need to ask for a raise if I have to supervise employees."

"You're not that indispensable," Dale joked. Joyce Phillips was his mother's age, the mother of one of his friends. He had had to struggle to overcome the urge to call her Mrs. Phillips when he had first hired her. She played surrogate mother to all of his employees, including him, looking out for them, checking in on them, asking how their families were, knowing their idiosyncrasies, likes and dislikes. She truly was indispensable. While he was the head of the business, she was the heart of the organization, keeping everything running smoothly. She was not happy about sharing her domain.

"Don't worry, Joyce. It will just be for a while, just long enough to give her some work experience so she can get a job." Kathleen for her part set about to win Joyce over as she tried to show both Joyce and Dale what she could do; how indispensable she could be. She learned the billing system and developed a website for the business and set up an account on Facebook.

"You have to have your image out there in the public if you want to grow your business. It's not enough to have an ad in the yellow pages any more. People are going on-line for their business needs. You have to keep up with the times," she had insisted. Dale had been impressed despite himself.

"Can you do this for Joy's studio as well?" he asked.

"Sure little brother, but it will cost you."

"Show me what you have and then we'll talk money." Joy had not yet developed a website for her dance studio. So far she had relied on word of mouth and more traditional advertising to bring in students. She liked it the way it was, didn't want to get too big, too fast, and yet understood the need to keep changing and growing if she wanted to stay in business. She just never had the time to pursue social media, especially most recently.

When Dale suggested having Kathleen set up a website, Joy balked.

"I don't know that I'm ready for that." It felt overwhelming at this point with everything else she was dealing with.

"It's a great idea, Joy," Sara had chimed in. "I've got a website and I don't even have a client base. You've got to have a website and a presence on social media. It doesn't take that much to keep it going once you get it set up, especially if you do it right. I can help maintain it once it's set up."

"Okay," Joy agreed, "but I want input on how it's set up." Joy didn't know that she had the brain power to invest in this right now. Her brain had been muddied by radiation. She was just starting her seven weeks of radiation. While not as bad as chemo, it left her exhausted most days. She hoped to have the bulk of her treatments done by the time classes started in late September. She was delaying the start of classes as long as possible to get her feet back on the ground but couldn't delay longer than that without risking the loss of students who might go elsewhere. Setting up this website might demand more of her than she was up to, and yet it gave her something else to think about besides cancer, so maybe it was what she needed. Nice to exercise her brain muscles on something besides cancer.

Esther and Sara were both on board in regards to the website and using social media to market her studio.

"I don't know a lot about social media but I do have some ideas for your studio if you are interested," Esther had said.

Joy sat down with Sara and Esther to brainstorm what she wanted in regards to a website. Sara came with design ideas and possible logos for branding her business.

"Branding, isn't that for cattle?" Joy asked.

"You have a brand whether you know it or not. In that you have a business, you have a brand. What you want to do is to be intentional about your brand, be aware of how you appear in the public eye."

"Where did you learn this, little sister?" Joy was surprised by Sara's confidence in this area.

"I took classes on marketing as part of my design major. Anyone in the business of creating logos needs to understand about branding."

Joy had never thought about branding. She had only wanted to dance and share her love of dancing with others.

"We need to start with a mission statement. It needs to be clear, catchy and easy to remember," Sara said. They sat up late into the night, throwing out ideas, working on a mission statement and laughing.

"It needs to be broad enough to leave room for growth, yet focused enough to capture the heart of what you are about," Sara had instructed.

"Have you thought about expanding?" Esther asked.

"Expanding? I'm barely hanging on."

"All the more reason to look at different options without going too broad. What are your dreams for the studio?" Sara jumped in.

"I don't know. Right now I'm having a hard time thinking beyond one day at a time, getting beyond this cancer."

"Then let us prime the pump. Let us dream with you," Esther said.

It had been what she needed. Funny how your goals change when confronted with a cancer diagnosis. She had gone from dreaming for the future to living just for the day, just for the next milestone. First it had been giving birth, then the mastectomy, now it was getting through radiation, but Sara and Esther were inviting her to look beyond, to realize she had a life beyond cancer and maybe, just maybe, she could start to make plans beyond surviving cancer, maybe she could dream again.

When they called it a night, they had settled on the tag line, Dancing for the Lord. The logo Joy decided on featured her name, Joy, in large, dancing letters in the middle, encircled by the words, School of Dance. Their mission statement was: Teaching love of dance and love of the Lord. Simple yet it said it all, said what Joy was about. It also left room for expansion into adult classes and other forms of dance, even belly dancing if they wanted.

"You could also start a blog about dance, about your faith, about your struggle with cancer. Let people know more about you. This will add interest, give people a reason to come back to your website," Sara suggested, repeating what Larry had told her.

Armed with the results from their brainstorming session, they met with Kathleen the next afternoon to give her what they had come up with and discuss particulars in regards to the website.

"Do you have everything you need?" Joy asked when they finished.

"And then some," Kathleen joked. "No, it's fine. I'd rather have a lot to work with than not enough. I don't know how to do logos and art work so it's good you have that. I'll work on this and see what I come up with. Oh, what about the color scheme? Did you have anything in mind?" Kathleen jotted down notes on the laptop Dale had loaned her to use for work. She was looking forward to the day when she would be able to buy her own top of the line computer, but for now this would do.

Joy, Sara and Esther looked at each other and laughed. How could they have forgotten something so basic?

"Maybe sky blue," Joy suggested. "Sara, you're the artist, what do you suggest?"

"Shades of pinks, reds, and yellows, suggesting passion and dance," Sara suggested.

"I'll see what I can do," Kathleen said, picking up her notes and the notes they had given her.

Kathleen was anxious to do well. A lot was riding on this. She had to prove herself not just to her family, but to herself. She had to know there was something she could do legally to bring in an income. She was determined not to live in her mom's basement any longer than necessary. That meant being gainfully employed. What she was doing at Dale's was okay, but she didn't want to do it forever, didn't want to be beholden to her brother, besides the fact that she wasn't getting paid.

Dale had liked her work on the website and had paid her for that, but there really wasn't enough work to justify hiring someone else. Kathleen had a hard time finding work to keep her busy the few hours she was there each day. But she was getting to know her brother through the process and finding this process surprisingly nice. She hadn't come back with dreams of repairing bridges she had broken long ago. She had figured that was unlikely, yet here she was doing just that, tentatively erecting a structure where once there had been none, a structure to allow communication between her and her brother. And now, with this next project, she had added more boards, opening a way to connect with his wife, his sister-in-law, and their mother.

Now if she could just connect with her sons. That had been what she had been most concerned about in coming back to her home town. She had even contemplated being re-united with them and skipping town, taking them with her. She had not realized the extent of damage eight years in prison could do to a relationship, especially when it included those vital formative years. She was mother only in name. The true mother to her boys was her own mother. She had known that for a long time, still there was a place inside her that had hoped it wasn't true, had hoped there was room for her in her son's lives.

"You know, mom, now that I've got my license, I can do more of the running for you. I can take Josh and Scot places. I can run to the store for groceries."

"I appreciate your offer, but Josh and Scott are pretty good about getting themselves where they need to go on their bikes." When Esther saw the look on Kathleen's face, she added, "But I will take you up on getting groceries and if something comes up with the boys, I'll let you know."

"Thanks, mom. I'm just trying to be helpful. I don't want to be a drain on the family."

"You aren't a drain," Esther said and was surprised to realize she meant it. She was slowly getting used to having her first-born around, allowing herself to relax in Kathleen's company and trusting that maybe, just maybe, she had changed.

Josh was a harder sell. Kathleen looked for ways to relate. She drove to his ball practices when she had time on her hands.

"You want to drive back with me? We can put your bike in the car," Kathleen had suggested only to be rebuffed.

"No, thanks, mom, I'd just as soon ride my bike," he said and turned back to talk to his friends.

"That your mom?" one asked.

"Yeah."

"Where has she been all this time?"

"Just away. Nothing to talk about. You want to meet up tonight?"

"Sure, might as well enjoy our freedom while we can."

Josh had wanted to see his mom but now that she was here he didn't know what to do with her. Grandma had been the one to take care of him. She was the one in charge. He didn't know how this other woman fit into his life, wasn't sure he wanted her in his life. It had hurt too much to have her leave before. He didn't want to get hurt again.

Chapter 32

Sara's hope for more work after her first small success wasn't realized. No more offers rolled in. She remained busy helping Joy out with the kids. It was good to be there but Sara knew it was just temporary. Time to kick the job hunt back into full gear, she told herself.

"Move to Detroit," Larry suggested. "There are lots of opportunities opening up and a great art scene." The thought was tempting. For all of its bad reputation, there were good things happening there. Urban farms, re-gentrification, regrowth spurred on by Dan Gilbert of Quicken Loans.

Larry had invited her for the weekend to show off the city. It had been fun, the Renaissance Center, Greek Town, the City Market, all of the different ethnic restaurants and of course, the Detroit Institute of Arts.

"First I would have to get a job, one that would pay the rent. Then I would have to find an apartment I could afford. I'm not sure about living alone in this city." Despite the improvements, Detroit was still Detroit, high crime rate, large pockets--no holes of poverty and the city in bankruptcy, no street lights at night, making an unsafe city even more unsafe.

"Maybe Anne would be interested in moving to Detroit?" Larry suggested. Anne was finishing out the year in their apartment. The lease ran from mid-August to mid-August, following the school year. Sara had been able to find someone to fill the remaining time on her lease, a friend who had been living in the dorm and needed a place for the summer before moving into her apartment for the fall. It had been an agreeable arrangement to Anne as well.

"She's not you," Anne said when they talked, "but I understand your need to be with your sister." Anne also had graduated without a job. She decided to stay in East Lansing until her lease was up. At least there she had her job cleaning the dorms in preparation for a new round of students. It paid the bills while she job hunted.

Living with Anne again was a dream, if they could find an apartment in a safe area they could afford and if they could find jobs.

They were two big ifs. Another draw was Larry. Their long-distance romance was not working. Sara wondered how Joy and Dale had managed all those years. She thought that if something didn't change, eventually Larry would lose interest and she would be back to square one, alone again. Still that wasn't enough to get her to move without a job. She had four months before she had to start paying on her student loans. She had to have something by then. As it was she was barely managing the expenses she had, her phone, incidentals and putting gas in the car her dad had bought her while in college. She was living rent free between Joy's home and her parents' home, but was feeling homeless and without roots.

Anne was preparing to move back home too, once her lease was up and her job over. They commiserated over margaritas and nachos at El Azteco, one of their favorite hang-outs, when Sara drove to East Lansing to visit.

"With no job I don't really have an option," Anne said. "I wouldn't mind staying in the area if I could just find a job. Maybe we should go to grad school?" Anne suggested.

"And pile student loans higher and deeper till we won't be able to dig our way out till in our graves? No, not for me. Besides, my parents helped me this far. I don't know that they will continue to support me unless I change into a more practical area of study." Sara stopped to pull a nacho chip out of the pile in front of her, allowing the cheese to hang off in long strings. "Mmmm, I love nachos. What were we talking about?"

"Grad school. Have you heard anything from Jeff?"

"I have. Seems he's going to law school in Detroit, U of D."

"Maybe we could share an apartment with him?" Anne teased.

"Yeah, my parents would love that, sharing an apartment with my gay, ex-boyfriend. I don't know what they would hate more, the fact that he is gay, or that he is a former boyfriend." It did give Sara another Detroit connection if she could find a job.

Sara was surprised to see Esther sitting with Joy when she got back, both with big grins on their faces.

"What are you two smiling about?"

"Come and see," they said, taking her by the hand and leading her out to Esther's car. They had been working all week, getting the studio ready for fall classes. They still had time before classes actually began but would be having an open house in a few weeks and had already started registering students for the fall. Sara thought they had just wanted to show her the progress they had made till she walked down the hall and saw her sketches lining the wall, then in a prominent space was her oil painting, next to an open door. On the door was a sign, Sara's Stylings. Inside was a spacious clean room, equipped with a desk and chair.

"We didn't know what all you would want in here. We thought it best to leave that to you, but the space is yours if you want it, a welcome addition to Joy's School of Dance," Joy said as Sara looked around.

Sara wasn't sure what to say. She didn't want to disappoint them by not sharing in their excitement, but wasn't sure that this was what she wanted. It would tie her to her hometown, not a bad thing, but was it right for her, she wondered.

"It's great," she said.

"You don't like it," Joy responded.

"No, no, it's just, I don't have any customers. I don't have any money. I can't afford lights and electricity much less rent."

"Who said anything about rent and utilities? You can have the space rent-free for as long as you want. And if you need any help with the business end of your studio, Esther here will take care of it. Who knows? This old building could become a hub for artistic activity. We could clean out those rooms in the basement that are just filled with dust and junk and invite other local artists to set up shop. What do you think?"

"I don't know what to say," Sara said.

"Thank you, would work," Joy said with a smile, hugging her sister. Esther could tell Sara wasn't as excited as they were.

"Why don't you think it over? Let us know when you know. It's not like we are going to rent the space to anyone else right now," Esther said.

"Thank you," Sara said. So much to think about, she thought, her head swimming.

Chapter 33

"You want fries with that?" Kathleen hated her job, but it was a job. Had she really sunk this low? She had thought jail was low, but this? The only job she had been able to get was at the local McDonald's and that was only because with the school year starting they needed someone to work week days. She dreaded running into anyone she knew from high school.

"Kathleen?"

"Yeah, did you want fries with that order?"

"Kathleen Reese?"

"Yes."

"You don't recognize me, do you?"

"No, should I?"

"Jack Trimble. We went to high school together."

"Oh, sure," she didn't remember him.

"You don't remember me," he said with a smile. "That's okay. We weren't exactly friends. You were busy with your friends and I was busy with mine. I didn't know you were back home. Last I heard you had moved to Chicago."

"Yeah, well I'm back." What remained unsaid was what she had been doing all those years.

"Well, it's good to see you. Maybe I'll see you around."

Now she hated her job even more. She had to go someplace where no one knew her. This was just the beginning. She had avoided looking up her old friends from high school, had lost touch with them when she had moved and saw no reason to reconnect now that she was back. Maybe they too had moved on to other places. Only losers had stayed and she had no desire to hang out with losers, this coming from the thirty-five year old behind the McDonald's counter. She saw the irony in the situation. All the more reason to leave, she assured herself. She had done what she had set out to do, had reconnected somewhat with her sons; now it was time to leave. She didn't know what was holding her here.

"So, how's it going?"

"How do you think it's going? I'm living in my mom's basement, working at McDonald's and my kids hate me."

"Why do you say that?" her probation officer leaned back in his chair.

"Because they do. They hardly talk to me since I've been back, or at least Josh won't talk to me. Scott's okay."

"It takes time. You can't just waltz into a child's life after eight years and expect to pick up where you left off. You have to rebuild trust."

"I don't know what I expected. I hate it here."

"So leave."

"Aren't you supposed to encourage me to stay, tell me I can't leave?"

"And would that do any good?"

"No."

"So why don't you leave?"

"I ask myself that almost every day. Maybe I will."

"Okay. All I ask is that you tell me where you are going so we can find you a new probation officer."

Kathleen just grunted in response. He wasn't like she had expected. She had expected him to be like the juvenile workers she had dealt with in high school. He wasn't like the probation officers she had dealt with after her earlier arrests. He was different. She didn't like it. She didn't like anyone right now.

Her mom liked him though. That would have been an immediate strike against him when she was a teenager. She was no longer a teenager. She disliked him for her own reasons.

He had come to her home to check out where she was living and had met her mom.

"Peter Blake," he had introduced himself, extending his hand.

"I'm Kathleen's mom, Esther."

"I figured as much."

"Have we met before?"

"I worked in the juvenile system back when Kathleen was a teenager. Maybe we met then."

Loser, Kathleen had thought, still working in this town after all these years. Maybe that was why she disliked him.

"You look familiar," Esther said, still holding his hand.

"Anyway, good to meet you." Peter paused, briefly meeting her gaze before he withdrew his hand.

"You, too. Do you have family?"

"My kids are grown and on their own. Their mother and I divorced ten years ago. It's just me now." Esther had noticed the lack of a wedding ring. "Maybe I'll see you around," he said as he left. Esther had been disappointed when she hadn't seen him around, but not surprised.

Chapter 34

Esther liked what she was doing at Joy's so much that she decided to start taking classes at the local community college, working towards an associate's degree in business administration, perhaps even transferring to a four-year institution if all went well.

"Go for it, grandma. Why does college just have to be for the grandkids?" Josh asked. "You've been telling me all along to plan on college. Maybe now it's your turn."

"That's right, mom," Kathleen chimed in. "I know you were disappointed when Dale and I didn't get a college degree. Maybe you are supposed to be the first one in the family to get that degree."

"But what about the money?"

"You still have the money in the trust from when grandpa died," Josh suggested.

"That's for you and Scott."

"You get your degree and with what you make with your new career you can help them with college," Kathleen said. "Besides, originally the money was to be for me. I want you to use the money for you."

"That's right, grandma. Think about yourself for once," Josh added.

"I'm with the kids on this," her dad added his two cents worth as they discussed it over a family dinner. "I wish I had the money to help you with this, but I'll try to do more around the house to make this possible."

"What about you, Scott?" Esther asked the youngest.

"Do it, grandma. I don't want to go to college anyway."

"Now wait a minute. I'll have no such talk," Esther started as everyone laughed.

"Besides, mom, you'll be setting a good example for Josh and Scott," Kathleen added.

"What about you? Why don't you take some classes too?" Esther asked.

"Yeah, mom, why don't you?" Josh and Scott both chimed in. "Just think about what a good example that would be," Josh added.

"I don't know," Kathleen tried to put them off.

"I'm sure there's enough money for both of us to go to community college," Esther persisted.

Kathleen looked around the table at the insistent faces and laughed. "Okay, okay. It won't hurt to try."

Secretly Kathleen had been thinking about going to school. The taste for learning she had discovered while in prison had turned from a craving into a hunger. She just didn't know how to go about satisfying that hunger, didn't think college would ever be an option for her. She knew she had blown her chance when she was younger and didn't feel she deserved a second chance. She had not once mentioned the trust money from her dad's insurance claim since being home. She had figured it had been spent on her sons. It had been a surprise to her to find out it had not been spent but she never mentioned using it. That was for Josh and Scott, not for her. So she had resigned herself to not going to school. No money -- no school.

She had met with a prison social worker before being discharged. She had encouraged Kathleen to go to college.

"You've done well while here. You show an aptitude for learning. I'd hate to see that not developed. There are programs available, loans and scholarships you could apply for if you want to go to school."

Kathleen had not responded, brushing her off as she prepared to leave. The social worker took her by the shoulder, stopping her. "Kathleen, don't blow it. You don't belong here. You more than most have the ability to make it on the outside. I don't expect to see you back here," she said.

Kathleen had walked out. "That makes two of us," she said to herself. No way would she be coming back, but she had her own ideas about how she would make that a reality. School hadn't been one of them. That was changing now.

The social worker had sent her recommendations in all of the paperwork that followed Kathleen to her probation officer.

"It says here that you took a couple of college-level computer classes while in prison and showed a capacity for learning. Have you considered going to college?" her probation officer had asked at their initial meeting.

"Look, right now all I want to do is reconnect with my kids, get my feet on the ground and some money in my pocket, then I'll be out of here."

"You know wherever you go, you will still be on probation?"

"I know, I know the routine. I have to check in with a probation officer, whether it be you or someone else, someplace else." Kathleen didn't know why she was being so difficult with this particular probation officer. She knew how to play the game. She knew the right things to say. She knew how to use the system to her advantage. How else did she manage to get all of this good time? He just rubbed her the wrong way. She walked in the door and felt like a rebellious teenager again. She knew this was not good, yet she did it anyway. That rebellious teenager had gotten her into way too much trouble in the past. She needed to relegate her to the past, needed to be an adult.

"If you change your mind about school, let me know. You may qualify for some assistance, at least government loans and grants."

"Yeah, yeah, so are we done?"

Thinking about this conversation Kathleen added, "I'll do it, but I want to pay my own way. I'll see what kind of assistance I qualify for. Any money I do take out of the trust fund, I'll pay back with interest. I'll consider it a loan. Deal?"

"Deal," all agreed.

At her next meeting with her probation officer, Kathleen told him her plan and asked for his assistance.

"I'll set up on appointment with the financial aid people at the college. They'll be able to help you," he said. "That's great news. I'm glad you are taking this step," he told her as he stood up to let her out the door.

"Well, I can't work at McDonald's the rest of my life."

"Some people do, but I think you know that's not right for you," he said as he held the door open for her.

Mother and daughter signed up for classes together. They both qualified for federal assistance but only if they went full-time, which was a minimum of three classes. There was significantly less assistance for part-time.

"I can't go full-time, not if I'm to continue helping Joy, and there's your grandpa and the boys to consider."

"You aren't going to back out now are you?" Kathleen asked. Esther had been thinking about just that. What was she doing going back to school in her fifties?

"Look, mom, if I can do it, so can you."

"But you are younger than me. You go full time. I'll take care of John and Scott."

"Neither of us is getting any younger. You are not getting out of this so easy! We are in this together. We can work it out." Kathleen signed up for night classes because of her day-time work schedule. Esther signed up for morning classes, leaving her afternoons and evenings open for helping Joy and working at the Dance studio. Joy had appreciated her help with the books so much that she decided to turn that aspect of her business over to Esther permanently, giving her a job.

"You don't have to pay me," Esther had balked at the idea. "I'm just happy I can help out."

"But you need a job and I need a business administrator. If you don't take the job, I'll have to hire someone else, someone I would have to train. You would be doing me a favor. Besides, who's going to implement all those great new ideas if I'm tied down with paper work? I'm still not back to full strength and won't be until this radiation is done, but once it's done, I'll need the help to free me to expand the business. What do you say?"

Esther had no option but to agree. It felt good to be gainfully employed again, even if only part-time. The part-time work fit her schedule, giving her time for school.

Chapter 35

"What do you think?" Larry had talked her into submitting an application at his place of employment. "I'm just a small cog in this big machine, but I'll put in a good word for you."

"I haven't gotten a job offer yet. And if I do get one, I don't know about leaving Joy just yet. Will it pay enough to cover the expenses of living in Detroit? I just don't know." Larry knew better than to offer to let her move in with him. It was too soon for both of them, besides the fact that he knew where Sara stood on this. Sara, for her part, almost wished he were pushing for that. After the incident with Jeff last year, she wondered that Larry wasn't pushing for more. They had long passed the third date. She remembered an episode of a sit-com about the third-date rule. Sex was expected at the third date. If you didn't have sex by then you fell into the friend category. She had considered it crazy at the time, still she wondered.

"What's so bad about falling into the friend category?" Joy asked when Sara had mentioned it.

"Well, the thought is that if you don't have sex by the third date you never will. You just end up friends."

"Is that dating according to Seinfeld?" Joy asked, mentioning a popular sitcom that was still in re-runs.

"Well, yeah."

"If young people start getting their dating advice from sitcoms, the world is in real trouble," Joy commented with a shake of her head. "What's wrong with being friends? Is Larry pressuring you?"

"No, not at all. That's the problem. Maybe he's just not that into me. Maybe he's not interested in me in that way. Maybe this relationship is another dead end."

"That's a lot of maybes."

"I know, but after what happened last year with Jeff, I can't help but wonder."

"The best marriages are between friends, either friends who fall in love, or people who fall in love and eventually become friends. It can happen either way. I think the three-date rule is a recipe for disaster. That works if all you are interested in is a sex partner. It doesn't work if what you are interested in is a life-partner, someone you can spend the rest of your life with. Think about it. That's a long time. You want to choose wisely. Marriage isn't easy, even when it's with the right person, when it's with your best friend."

"You and Dale make it seem easy."

"That's all you see. We have our share of struggles. Do you think it was easy, those eight years we were living in separate cities? We almost broke up several times."

"Why didn't you?"

"Because he was my best friend. I couldn't stand to lose my best friend, and he felt the same way. We always came back to each other. And then, once we were married do you think it was easy to adjust to each other's idiosyncrasies? Do you think it's easy, being with someone day in and day out? We thought the biggest challenge to our relationship was distance. We thought that once we were in the same city, everything would work out, there would be no more misunderstandings and disagreements; but see, sometimes, the distance can make it easier to avoid subjects you don't want to address. I've known couples who survive years of separation only to break up when they are back together in the same town. The distance had helped them hide the problems between them and how they had grown apart."

"So why didn't that happen to you?"

"Dale knows I would kill him if he broke up with me," Joy teased. "No," she said with a laugh, smiling at her little sister. "Because we were friends first, and yet we kept that spark too. We knew what we wanted, shared the same values. Even then there are disagreements, but none we couldn't work out. In the end, we knew we wanted to be together, knew there was no one else we would rather spend our lives with," Joy paused before continuing.

"You know, relationships are balancing acts. It's knowing when to be together and when to be apart, knowing how to be apart while together, sharing the same space, giving each other space, but also knowing when to come together again. I didn't want to live like mom."

"Me neither."

"It's not that I'm trying to put her down or her marriage. If it works for her, fine – but it just seems she gave up everything in marriage to be the wife dad expected. If you give up too much, you can become enmeshed, you can lose yourself in an unhealthy way. I sometimes wonder who mom is without dad."

"But isn't that what marriage is about, two becoming one, finding yourself by dying to yourself? That's what the church tells us."

"It's a balancing act. How can you die to yourself if you don't first have a self to give? If you don't know who you are, how can you be in relationship with anyone else? And it has to be a mutual self-giving. If it's mutual then you are both giving to each other and finding yourself in the process. If it's one-sided, then one person does all of the giving and becomes lost in the other person. It's not my idea of what I want in a marriage."

"That sounds like mom and dad."

"Maybe, but we don't know, do we? If it works for them . . . I've learned to be careful about judging other people's relationships, just as I try not to judge others."

"If it's so hard, then why bother, why get married at all?"

"Because nothing truly good in this life comes without work and struggle. The things we value the most aren't necessarily what we've been given, but what we work for. And the benefits of a good marriage far outweigh the struggles. I have someone who loves me and whom I love, someone to share my life with me. Someone who will be there when others are gone, when the kids have grown and have lives of their own. Someone who knows me better than anyone else, and loves me anyway. It's worth the work."

"I never would have guessed you and Dale had any disagreements. You make it look easy."

"That's because we keep our disagreements between us. They are not for others to see. You know, dance isn't easy. It takes years of practice, hard work and discipline, daily practice and keeping yourself in shape, yet the best dancers when they are on stage, they make it seem easy. They float. Just look at Fred Astaire and Ginger Rogers. They dance together so effortlessly, they make it look easy, but if you or I were to try to do the same dance, we would probably trip over our feet. It takes a lot of work to make it look easy." Joy paused while Sara tried to take it all in.

"So, how about you and Larry? What's happening there?"

"Not much, not with the distance and seeing each other so rarely. Maybe that's why he wants me to move to Detroit, to give the relationship a chance. And maybe that's why I'm hesitant to move. I don't know whether I want to give this relationship a chance."

"Why not? You won't know until you give it more time."

"Maybe."

"Do you want this to be the relationship you regret because you never gave it a chance?" Joy asked while getting up and yawning. "Time for bed. The kids will be up before I know it."

Chapter 36

"What's up?" Kathleen asked Esther, responding to the voice message left on her phone. "I'm on break. I've only got a few minutes."

"Dale and Joy had to take baby Grace to the ER. She has a fever of 106. I'm here with the kids but I've got a class tonight at six. Could you come over after your shift and watch Ashley and Jacob?"

"Where's Sara?"

"She's spending the weekend with friends in Detroit. I'd ask Josh but I know he's planning on going to the game. Can you do it?"

"Sure. I get off at five. I'll come over after that. See you then." Kathleen was concerned about watching Ashley and Jacob. She had not spent much time with them since getting back. She didn't know the first thing about taking care of small children. She had not done much babysitting as a teenager, and Josh and Scott – well, that was another story. Why should two small kids fill her with fear and trembling, she wondered.

"They're eating dinner right now. All you have to do is clean up and get them to bed," her mom told her as she hurried out the door. "I'll call you on my break to see how it's going. Bed time is seven-thirty," Esther called back to her as she went out the door.

"Okay," Kathleen said as she hung up her coat. She hadn't changed out of her uniform yet. She cautiously approached the two who were sitting at the kitchen table. "So, how are you?"

"Jacob spit his peas at me," Ashley complained.

"Oh, he did. Jacob, that's not nice." Jacob giggled, clearly thinking this was the funniest game yet in his three years of life. He picked up some more peas and threw them at his sister, laughing the whole time.

"Jacob, stop that," Kathleen said as she removed what remained of his peas from his plate. He spit what was in his mouth at her. "That's not funny," she said.

"Yes it is," he giggled.

"Are you done?"

"Yes."

"Okay, let me clean you up then you can come down."

"I'm done, too, Aunt Kathleen," Ashley said.

"But you've hardly touched your food." Kathleen looked at the full plate of mashed potatoes, peas and chicken strips.

"I'm not hungry."

"No dessert if you don't clean your plate."

"I ate a chicken strip."

"That's not enough. You have to eat some peas and potatoes."

"I'm not hungry!" Ashley insisted. Kathleen was afraid she was getting herself into an all-out food war. No wonder Jacob had thrown his peas at her. She felt like doing that too.

"Okay, just get down."

"Can we watch a video?"

"Yes, just let me clean up first." Kathleen took a couple of spoonsful of Ashley's mashed potatoes and ate the remaining chicken strip. "Not terrible," she said scraping the peas into the garbage. She changed out of her uniform before getting ready to go into the front room.

In the front room she could hear the sound of crying. Jacob came running into the kitchen.

"What's the matter?" Kathleen asked, picking up the weeping toddler.

"Ashley took my toy," he sobbed.

Kathleen walked into the front room. "Ashley, did you take Jacob's toy?" She saw Ashley playing with Jacob's spinning top.

"No, this is my toy. It was my toy before it was Jacob's."

"You're too old for that. Why don't you let Jacob have it back?"

"Because it's mine."

"Ashley," Katherine said with what she hoped was a threatening tone. "Give Jacob back his toy or go to your room."

"Fine. Here's your stupid toy," Ashley said, throwing the toy at Jacob, missing his head.

What to do, Kathleen thought. Pick your battles, she told herself. Let this one go, she decided.

"Who wants to watch Little Mermaid?" she asked, thinking Ashley would respond. Ashley sat on the couch pouting.

"Peter Pan," Jacob stated.

"Okay, Peter Pan it is," Kathleen said. She put the video in and went back to cleaning the kitchen.

She was surprised by a small voice.

"I hate Baby Grace," Ashley said. Kathleen turned around to face the small child.

"Why, Ashley?"

"Because she made mommy sick."

"Baby Grace didn't make mommy sick."

"Is Baby Grace going to die?" Ashley asked.

"No," Kathleen said, squatting down so she could look straight into Ashley's face. "No, she's not going to die. What makes you think so?"

"She's so sick. Mommy and daddy are worried. I don't want her to die."

"She's at the hospital. The doctors will make her all better."

"I wanted her to die when mommy was sick. She was making mommy sick. But now I don't want her to die."

"Baby Grace didn't make mommy sick."

"Then why is mommy so sick?" Kathleen picked Ashley up and sat her in her lap. How to explain cancer to a five year old? "There's something bad growing inside your mommy. The doctors are killing those bad cells so the good cells can grow."

"Baby Grace was growing inside mommy." What to say, Kathleen struggled.

"Yes, baby Grace grew inside mommy but she didn't make mommy sick."

"I miss my mommy."

"She'll be home soon."

"And Baby Grace?"

"She'll be home too."

"I don't want mommy to be sick anymore."

"I know. I want your mommy to get better too. She is getting better. All we can do is pray for your mommy. She is getting better and Baby Grace is going to be okay too. You want ice cream?" Kathleen said, deciding now was not the time to enforce the no-dessert rule.

"Uh huh," Ashley nodded her head.

"Okay, you go watch Peter Pan with your brother and I'll be right there with the ice cream."

Kathleen watched the video with Ashley and Jacob then got them ready for bed. She tucked Ashley in and prepared to turn out the light.

"What about prayers?"

"What?"

"We haven't said prayers yet."

"Oh, okay, go ahead."

"You have to pray with us."

"Okay, what do I do?"

"I'll help you, fold your hands and bow your head," Ashley instructed. "God bless mommy and daddy and Jacob and Baby Grace. And God, please make mommy and Baby Grace all better," Ashley prayed. "Oh, and God bless Aunt Kathleen."

"Is that it?" Kathleen asked.

"Yes, you can open your eyes now," Ashley told her.

"Okay, now you go to sleep. Your mom and dad will be home when you wake up," she said giving Ashley a kiss.

"Me, too," Jacob said.

"You need a kiss, too?"

"Uh huh," Jacob nodded his head. Kathleen smiled, leaned over and gave him a kiss. "Now go to sleep you two."

Dale came home around ten.

"Joy stayed in the hospital with Grace."

"How is she?"

"She's dehydrated from the fever. They are giving her IV fluids and trying to get her fever down. She'll be okay once they get the fever down. Thank you for coming over."

"Any time, little brother, any time. They are good kids. Do you need someone to come back tomorrow?"

"Yes, if you would. I want to go back tomorrow to relieve Joy. I'll call you in the morning."

Esther was getting home about the same time that Kathleen got home.

"How did it go? How's Grace?"

"They are keeping her overnight until her fever goes down. Joy is staying with her. I told Dale I would come back in the morning so he can go to the hospital."

"That's okay, I can go tomorrow. How did it go with the kids?"

"Okay. They're good kids. Not that much older than Dale and I were when dad died."

"Yeah, I know."

"You know, Ashley thinks she caused Grace to be sick. She said she had wanted her dead because she was making mommy sick."

"So what did you tell her?"

"That she hadn't made Grace sick and that Grace hadn't made mommy sick. How do you explain cancer to a five year old?"

"That I don't know," Esther sat down with Kathleen.

"You know, I think I thought I caused dad's death," Kathleen said hesitantly.

"What do you mean? It was an accident at work. You were just four. You had nothing to do with your dad's death."

"But I had been mad at him. He had sent me to my room for picking on Dale. I was mad at him and told him I hated him."

"Oh, honey, why didn't you say anything before this?"

"Because I didn't remember it until Ashley told me how she hated baby Grace. I think I really believed I caused dad's death."

"Of course you didn't, you know that don't you? And your dad knew you loved him."

"Did he, how could he when the last thing I told him was I hate him?"

"Because he knew you were just angry. Your dad loved you."

"I don't deserve his love. I don't deserve anyone's love," Kathleen said, lowering her head into her hands.

"You know that's not true."

"Do I? I guess in my head I know it. In my heart though, I know I'm not loveable. Who would love me?"

"I do, Kathleen, and your dad did." Esther sat quietly, waiting for Kathleen to respond.

"And that's not the worst of it," she finally said, "the worst of it is that I look at Ashley and Jacob and I realize what I missed out on by not being there for Josh and Scott. There's nothing I can do about it. There's no going back, no making it up to them." Kathleen fought back tears.

Just then Josh came through the door.

"What's wrong, mom?"

"Nothing," Esther answered for her. "How was the game?"

"Lame. We lost. I'm going to bed."

"Okay."

Josh paused and added, "You sure you're okay, mom?"

"I'm sure," Kathleen managed. "How much do you think he heard?" she asked when Josh was safely out of hearing range.

"I don't know." The moment broken, Esther didn't know how to get it back.

"Well, guess I'll go to bed too," Kathleen said.

Esther took her hand and said, "You can't change the past but you can make the future better, for yourself and your sons."

"Yeah, sure, goodnight, mom," Kathleen said, but there was no good night for her as she tossed and turned.

Chapter 37

"Dale just called," Esther said the following morning. "Grace's fever has broken; she's almost fully re-hydrated and will be released later this morning. I'm going over so Dale can pick up Joy and the baby. Do you want to come with me?" she asked Kathleen when she came upstairs from the basement.

"No, no thanks," she responded.

"Are you okay? You don't look so good."

"I'm fine. Didn't sleep too well last night. I've got a lot of studying to do. I might go to the library and study."

"Okay, as long as you're okay." Esther was hesitant to leave Kathleen alone after last night. Once again, torn between her two children, she thought. How can she choose? She had to take Kathleen at her word and trust that she was okay even though her gut told her it wasn't so.

Kathleen poured herself a cup of coffee and took it downstairs so she could continue to work out the plan she had developed during her sleepless night. It wasn't as clear to her in the light of day as it had been during the dark. That she was leaving was clear to her; how to do this was what was unclear. Does she take her grandfather's car and pay him back later when she had money? Or take the bus, leave the way she had come? Neither option seemed that good, especially since both were dependent on money she didn't have.

Money, how was she going to get money to fund her new life, she wondered. Maybe she could borrow money from her old contacts in Chicago. She knew it would come with a price. Was she ready to pay that price? She didn't know. What would she do? She didn't want to go back to her old life style. She wanted something different for herself, but she couldn't stay here.

She packed her few belongings, including her text books, took her grandpa's keys and started for the door.

"Where are you going young lady?" her grandfather stopped her.

"Just to the library. You don't mind, do you?" she said as she jangled his keys.

"Okay, but the gas tank better be full when you return."

Kathleen started out in the direction of the library, then turned. She knew where she was going now. She headed out of town to the cemetery. She hadn't been there since she had left the last time, over ten years ago. It had been the place she always went before leaving town, why should this time be different?

"Have you seen my mom?" Josh asked his great grandfather when he came downstairs.

"Yeah, she went to the library," he responded.

"No, she didn't. She's leaving again," he said, holding a letter in his hand. "Read this," he handed it to his great grandfather.

Dear Josh,

I have failed you again. I wasn't the mother you needed ten years ago and it seems I'm not the mother you need now. I'm so sorry. I'm sorry for leaving you years ago, and I'm sorry that I can't make it up to you now. But I'm glad to know you have another mother in grandma, a far better mother than I could ever be. I know that I have been a disappointment to all of the people I have loved and I'm sorry about that, too.

I just want you to know that despite how poorly I've shown it, I do love you and your brother, and I'm proud of you. Please tell Scott that for me.

Love,
Mom

"Where's grandma?" Josh asked after Erik finished reading.

"She's at your Uncle Dale's."

"We have to go find mom. Where is your car?"

"Your mom has it."

"We have to get grandma. She'll help us find her."

"What's up?" Scott asked as he came into the kitchen.

"Nothing, Scott," Josh told him, then said to his great grandfather, "I'll take care of this."

"No, it's not nothing," Scott insisted. "I can tell. You treat me like I'm a baby. I'm only two years younger than you."

"Okay," Josh stopped in his tracks, "Mom's gone. I'm going to look for her."

"Let me go too."

"No, you stay here with great grandpa. We need someone here in case she comes back," Josh insisted, knowing the lie behind his words. He knew she wasn't coming back, not on her own.

"Wait, Josh, let's call your grandma first."

Erik called Esther and filled her in on the events of the morning.

"I knew something was up," she said, sitting down as her dad read Kathleen's letter to her. "I knew I shouldn't have left her alone but Dale needed me."

"Don't blame yourself for Kathleen's actions. You couldn't stop her before this. You can't stop her now if she's determined to leave."

"How's Josh?"

"He wants to look for her."

"Tell him to wait until I get there. Dale should be home soon with Joy and the baby. I'll come as soon as he gets back." She hung up then looked through her purse for the business card she had tucked away months before. She dialed the number and was surprised when an actual voice answered.

"Officer Blake?"

"Yes," the voice responded.

"This is Esther, Kathleen Reese's mother."

"Is something wrong?"

"Yes, I think she's run off again."

"How long has she been gone?"

"Just since this morning but she left a note for her son saying she was leaving. What if she isn't leaving but hurts herself?"

"Do you have any idea where she might go?"

"Back to Chicago maybe. She has her grandfather's car ... but there is a place she might go first – to the cemetery, to her dad's grave." She remembered how Kathleen was drawn to her dad's grave as a teenager; how Kathleen had mentioned going to the cemetery before she had gone to Chicago.

"Where are you now?"

"I'm at my son's home babysitting. I can't leave until he gets back."

"Okay, I'll go by myself. I'll call you if I find anything."

Esther called back her dad and let him know what was happening. "I called Kathleen's probation officer. He's going to see if she went to Dale's grave. Put Josh on the phone, would you?"

"I can't. He left on his bike, said he wasn't going to just wait around here when his mom was missing."

"Great, so now we have both of them missing."

"Don't worry about Josh. He's got a good head on his shoulders. I'll take care of things here. I'll let you know if I hear anything."

"Thank you," Esther said as she put down the phone.

"What's wrong, grandma?" Ashley asked her.

"Nothing, honey. Here, let's get a snack. Your mom and dad will be home soon."

Josh wasn't sure where he was going, he just knew he had to do something, couldn't sit at home helpless as he had in the past when his mom had left. Then he had had no choice. Now he had a choice. It seemed to him that maybe she had gone to grandpa's grave. She had mentioned to him how as a teenager whenever she was in trouble she would go there and talk to grandpa. It was worth a try.

The cemetery was several miles from home. Josh pushed himself to keep going on this brisk autumn morning. He had left without any gloves, just grabbing a jacket and his helmet before taking off. While the rest of his body warmed from the exercise, his fingers were numb.

He pulled into the cemetery and saw his great grandfather's car parked in the back. He had been right, he told himself.

Kathleen sat on a bench near her dad's grave, thoughts swirling in her head. She had called one of her Chicago contacts and he had been happy to hear from her.

"Kathleen, it's good to hear from you. Where have you been? I heard you were released. How come you didn't call me?"

"I had some family business to take care of."

"You know, we are family, you're family to us. We always take care of our family. When you coming back? We'll set you up again."

"I don't know. Maybe tonight, maybe tomorrow. I'll call you when I know." But the minute she heard his voice she knew she didn't want to go back, not to that life, a life of petty crimes and drugs. But if not there, then what would she do?

"Hi, dad," she said to the grave marker, squatting down in order to touch its surface. "It's me, Kathleen. Seems it's been a long time. Here I am again. I've messed things up again. I don't know why I even bother, why I'm still alive. Why should I live when you are dead? Maybe everyone would have been better off if I had joined you before this. I don't know why God keeps me around." She remained in silence until a voice broke through the quiet.

"Mom," Josh said as he approached. Now that he was here he didn't know what to say. "What are you doing?"

Kathleen stood up and turned, shaking her head, "Josh, how did you find me?"

"Remember, you told me how you used to visit grandpa's grave."

"Oh, yeah, I guess I did. I didn't think you would remember, didn't think you were listening."

"Of course I was listening. I listened to everything you told me, I just didn't show it. I heard what you said last night, about not being able to make it up to us for leaving."

"Look, I'm sorry you heard that." She turned back around looking at her father's grave again.

"I'm not. What are you going to do?" Kathleen looked past the grave, staring beyond it, avoiding Josh's gaze.

"I don't know. Maybe go someplace where I can start over, where no one knows me."

"Why can't you do that here, start over?"

Kathleen paused and looked down at her dad's grave before responding, "You know that I just mess things up."

"Then take me with you."

"What?" Kathleen shook her head and turned to face him.

"You heard me, take me with you. Scott will be okay with grandma and great grandpa."

"I can't do that to them."

"Yet you'll leave all of us again."

A car pulled up alongside Kathleen's car. Peter got out but stood back a respectful distance to allow mother and son a chance to speak. Esther arrived shortly afterwards. He motioned to her to stay back. He saw mother and son hug. Then he approached.

"Kathleen, you wouldn't skip town without letting me know, would you? That was our agreement."

"Agreements are made to be broken, at least ones I make."

"Don't do this to us again," Esther said as she approached, unable to wait any longer. "You have no right to just show up, find a way into our hearts and then leave just when we thought you would stay. Just when I thought you had changed."

"Who's leaving? Can't a daughter pay her respects to her dad without everyone freaking out," Kathleen said with tears in her eyes. "I was going to leave, but it seems I've been found out. Josh here won't let me leave, not without him anyway, so I guess I have to stay."

Esther didn't know what had been said between mother and son, but whatever it was, Kathleen was staying. She was grateful for that.

"Is anyone hungry?" Officer Blake asked. "Let's get some lunch, my treat," he offered. Kathleen put Josh's bike in the back of her car and they followed Peter to a nearby restaurant. Esther called her dad and let him know what happened.

"We'll be home shortly."

Chapter 38

Sara had the best weekend. She and Anne had stayed at Jeff's apartment. It was like old times, the three of them hanging out together. Larry had been a welcome addition. He had fit right in. Sara was happy about that. Much as she enjoyed hanging out with the three of them, she was happy to have some time with Larry, just the two of them, on Sunday. Anne had left that morning. Jeff needed to study so that had left them alone. She had gone to church with Larry then out for lunch. Afterwards they had gone to a local park. Sara reveled in the memory of his kisses and his arms around her, keeping her warm in the autumn air. She had not wanted the day to end.

Sara went back to Larry's apartment with him before leaving. She was relieved to see that Larry's suitemate was gone.

"So, we have the place all to ourselves, you sly spider, luring me into your lair," she said with a smile.

"Well, if it works I am weaving a web to get you to stay," he said, drawing her closer.

"No, I have to go. Joy needs me. I have to watch the kids for her while she finishes her radiation and you have to work."

"Oh, yeah, that, but that's tomorrow," Larry said as they kissed. "Speaking of work, have you heard anything about your job application?"

"No, probably another dead end."

"Don't dismiss it so soon."

"Okay. I really have to be going," she said as she reluctantly pulled back. "I'll call you when I get home," she told him.

The idea of moving to Detroit didn't seem so far-fetched after the weekend. And she definitely wanted to see more of Larry. She relived the events of the last two days as she drove home, happily smiling inside. Her bubble of excitement burst when she got home and heard of all that she had missed.

"What, baby Grace in the hospital? And no one called me?"

"We didn't want to spoil your weekend. It all worked out. Kathleen helped out. But then Kathleen almost left. I think she's staying for good though."

"That's a relief, I guess," Sara said. She didn't know what to think, two major crises in one weekend. What else would she miss if she moved away? But then they had survived the crisis without her. Maybe she wasn't indispensable after all. She could be replaced, maybe already was being replaced by Kathleen. No reason to hang around here. She felt both relieved and disappointed. It was a relief to know she could leave if she wanted, but it was a disappointment to be so easily replaced. She didn't know that she wanted to miss out on any more crises in her family.

When she received a call for an interview for the job she had applied for, Sara didn't know whether to be excited or scared. What if she got the job? Then she would have to make a decision. She didn't know that she wanted to do that just yet.

The interview was scheduled for Thursday. She was going to have lunch with Larry afterwards, then would return home for the weekend. Joy was hosting another open house that weekend and needed her help.

"How soon could you start?" The interview had gone well. Sara didn't know what to say when they asked that question. Larry had prepared her for this but she still wasn't sure. It made it seem too real.

"Tell them you can start any time. We can worry about getting you a place later," he had told her.

"I would need time to find an apartment and move," Sara said instead, "maybe a month or two."

"We may need someone right away. Would you be able to commute for a while in order to start earlier?"

"I think so," she had said. The idea of a commute to Detroit was far from ideal but others did it, she guessed she could if she got the job.

"So how did it go?" Larry asked at lunch.

"Good, I think. They said I would hear back from them next week."

"In the meantime, I'll keep my eyes out for an apartment for you."

"Okay," she had agreed.

At the open house Sara was approached by several women who had been impressed by her art work. She gave out a number of her business cards yet was surprised when she actually received a commission for a painting and another one for a charcoal drawing the next day. She also had a job offer.

"Why did all of this have to happen at once?" she lamented to Joy.

"That's a good problem to have."

"Yes, but now I don't know what to do."

"What do you want to do?"

"If I knew that the answer would be simple. I would like to do more with my art but the chances of being able to support myself with it are not good."

"You don't have to support yourself just yet. You know you are always welcome here until you get your feet on the ground."

"I know." Sara also knew that she wasn't needed as much now. Joy had finished her last radiation treatment and would need less help as she got stronger. She was starting to feel like she was underfoot and in the way rather than being a help, though she knew Joy would never say so.

She could move back home with her parents. Her mother would welcome the company, she knew, but she wanted to be on her own as much as possible.

"The job would involve some creativity, graphic designs and marketing campaigns. There's room for growth and I like Detroit, and then there's Larry."

"Yes, Larry," Joy said with raised eyebrows.

"Stop, you already know all there is to know there."

"Can't you find all of this here?"

"I've tried, there are no jobs."

"I could use some help with marketing."

"Big sister, you can't put the whole family on your payroll."

"Dale could use your marketing advice as well."

"He has it, for free, both of you, any time you want."

"Sounds like you've made up your mind. What will I do with your studio space?"

"Don't give it away just yet. Maybe Kathleen could set up shop there?" Sara found herself suggesting even as she had told Joy to keep the space for her. Maybe she had decided, she thought.

"I think Sara is moving to Detroit," Joy told Dale that night once the kids were in bed.

"That's okay, we'll manage all right without her," he responded.

"I know that, but I'll miss her."

"I will too," he opened up his brief case. Joy thought he was going to look through papers while in bed. Instead he handed her a slip of paper. "I wrote this down several months ago. I had forgotten it was in my brief case until I cleaned it out today. It seemed appropriate." Joy read the paper: Joy is suffering that has been worked through. She looked up at Dale without a word; she knew she didn't have to speak.

"We will get through this the way we have every other challenge, together. I'm so glad I have my Joy back," he said, "together we can handle anything life throws at us."

Chapter 39

Sara was nervous about Thanksgiving this year. She was meeting Larry's family.

"Larry, do we have everything?" she asked as he picked her up at her apartment and loaded her bags into his car.

"We are only going to be gone two days, Sara. We've already been over this," he said with a smile. "How much do we need?"

They were spending Thanksgiving with her family then with his family the next day, then back to Detroit. Larry leaned over and kissed her before backing out of their parking spot. "Don't worry. My parents will love you. I'm the one who should be worried, meeting that tribe you call your family."

Joy was happily cancer free. Her last test came back with "No Evidence of Disease." NED. She hoped to be dating NED for the rest of her life. Classes were going well and she finally had the energy to start thinking about adding adult classes and expanding into classes on yoga, meditation and exercise for cancer patients, as Esther had suggested. Esther's classes were going well and she was excited about developing "Joy's Center for the Arts." Kathleen's classes were also going well as she settled in to life in her hometown. All reasons for giving thanks this year.

Joy talked her mom into having Thanksgiving at her home.

"Are you sure you are up for it?" her mom asked. "After all you've been through, I can handle Thanksgiving."

"It's because of all I've been through that I want to host Thanksgiving. I have so much to be thankful for. I want to share it with all of you. It's my way of thanking everyone for how great you were during my pregnancy and cancer. Let me do it. Besides, Esther will help and I'll expect you to help as well. It will be crowded but it will be family." Mary agreed.

"But Christmas is still mine," she insisted.

"Wouldn't have it any other way," Joy smiled.

Thanksgiving included Joy's family, Joy's brothers and their families and her parents, as well as Dale's family. It would be a tight squeeze but they would make it work.

"If you plan on this being a regular thing, maybe we better look at adding on," Dale told her as they set up a table and chairs throughout their living room.

Sara greeted Esther with a hug as she came in carrying a casserole, followed by Peter.

"I bought an extra person. I hope you don't mind," Esther said. "He was going to be alone over Thanksgiving so I insisted he come with us. I told him I had plenty enough family to share."

"My kids and their families are with their mom for Thanksgiving," Peter added. "I really appreciate the invite."

"There's always room for more," Joy said, giving Peter a hug. "We are happy to have you here." Joy and Dale were happy that Esther finally had a man in her life after so many years alone.

Kathleen came in followed by Josh and Scott, each carrying more food. Erick brought up the rear. Esther was happy to have her family together and even more to be dating Peter. They had started dating shortly after the cemetery incident. It was an off again, on again relationship but had promise. He was solid; a source of stability in her life that sometimes seemed out of control. She had come a long way since losing her job last year. She still was thrown off-balance at times but when that happened, she had Peter to lean on as a friend and more.

As Joy looked over the scene of her home overflowing with family, she felt balanced and secure. Who knew what other challenges might confront her, knocking her off balance? But for now she was at peace, dancing on the high wire we call life.

That night, Sara, Esther and Joy gathered after the dishes were washed and left-overs sent home with guests or safely stored in the refrigerator. Larry was busy playing with Joy's children. He fit in with ease, Sara thought with relief. Now to get through meeting his family tomorrow.

They opened a bottle of sparkling wine and thanked God for their many blessings as they clinked their glasses and said together, "Thus far, by grace!"

> "Happiness is not a matter of intensity
> but of balance and order and rhythm and harmony."
> *Thomas Merton*

Q&A on *Dancing on a High Wire*

Q – How did you come to write *Dancing on a High Wire*?

A – Through NaNoWriMo – National Novel Writing Month. This novel was different from my other novels. Each of these took me many years to finally complete and make ready for publication. Two of my novels, *Buying Time*, and, *Land of Deep Water*, I had written in part over thirty years ago during a time when novels poured out of me, one after another. I wrote nine novels during that period, most of which were not good. I kept the best of them for revising later.

I first heard about NaNoWriMo in the fall of 2013 while on a writing retreat at my brother's cottage. The idea intrigued me. I had never tried anything like this before. During my prolific period in my twenties, I wrote fast and furious. Still I don't believe that I wrote a whole novel in one month. Since I was semi-retired from ministry I thought, what would it hurt? Why not give it a try? I had an idea from my twenties that I wanted to develop. By the time I came home the idea for a story about women who have been knocked off balance by life circumstances had formulated in my brain.

I sat down in November and wrote *Dancing on a High Wire*. Because it didn't take the same amount of time that my other novels took, I was a little nervous about it. I worried whether there were any glaring plot or character mistakes. It has been through a copy edit and I've had others read it as I've done with my other books, so it's ready.

Q – How did you decide on your characters?

A – Sara: One of the novels from my twenties was based on the story of a friend of mine. When I first met him he had been engaged. Then the engagement was broken off because he had accepted he was gay.

His fiancé quickly started dating another man. I watched all of this transpire and felt there was a story worth telling.

The college years are often times of experimentation as students try out different majors, different lifestyles and identities, including sexual identity. I reflected on his former fiancé and how she might have reacted to his announcement. I knew my friend to be a devout Catholic and catechist. I knew this was not a decision he had taken lightly but that he had prayed about it, especially since it was much harder to be accepted back then, 1978.

I approached my friend about my idea and together we wrote the book, *Jack and Jean*. I wrote the first and third section, the story of their engagement, then Jean's story after the break-up. He wrote the middle section, Jack's story. I had kept the manuscript thinking I might use it as the basis of a story. I looked over parts of the manuscript in preparation for writing then threw it out and started anew, keeping only the basic story line. Thus the character of Sara was created.

Joy: Breast cancer is everywhere. A good friend of mine had had it a number of years ago and came out cancer free. More recently my children's step-mother underwent treatment for breast cancer. Then I heard about a friend's daughter who was pregnant and had been diagnosed with breast cancer. These individuals were my inspiration for the character Joy.

Esther: I worked for twelve years at a retirement community before my position was eliminated. Prior to this the community had gone from having its own food service to bringing in a company. A number of old timers lost their jobs from this. I also witnessed a number of other long time workers lose positions both before and after I did. These were the basis for my character, Esther. I wanted someone older to balance out my characters, one who had lost her job after over twenty-five years and had few other job opportunities.

Q – Are you planning on participating in NaNoWriMo again?

A – Definitely! This year I plan to write a sequel to *Dancing*, tentatively called, *Still Dancing*, picking up where the previous book left off. I'd like to keep doing this, each year focusing on different characters. In 2015 I'm planning on writing, *Slow Waltz*. So yes, my intent is to write a book each November.

Q – You address some difficult topics in this book, homosexuality and abortion. Did you find this difficult?

A – Yes. You might say I was doing a balancing act much as my characters were as I dealt with these issues. As previously mentioned, I had wanted to do more with the story from my college years. I knew it was a potentially volatile topic depending on how I handled it. Thirty five years later, the topic is less volatile but still worth exploring. Homosexuality was still coming out of the shadows in 1978. Now not only is it openly discussed, gay marriages are becoming a reality, something I would not have expected in college. I avoid the issue of gay marriage because it is currently such an explosive topic. I wanted to explore through Sara how homosexuality might challenge a person's sexual identity. I was afraid a discussion of gay marriage would have taken away from this.

Abortion is also an emotion-laden topic. Fortunately there are options available for pregnant women with breast cancer. If this had been written at another time Joy's decision would have been more difficult. I wanted a chance to explore more fully one woman's opposition to abortion when it meant endangering her own life.

Note to the reader:

Did you enjoy reading this book? If so, please leave a review on Amazon. Your comments would be appreciated and mean so much to me in terms of helping others notice my book. You, the reader, have the power to make or break a book in this day of emarketing and social media.

Thank you so much for reading *Dancing on a High Wire*. Stay tuned for the sequel!

Patricia Robertson

Other novels by Patricia M. Robertson

Dreamweavers – Dream again, wherever you are in your life. An exploration of how our dreams change over the course of our lifetime. Join Kate, a single mom, her teenage daughter, Terri, and others as they seek out new dreams for their life.

Buying Time – Visit the peace movement during the Cold War era of Ronald Regan, SDI (Strategic Defense Initiative) and MAD (Mutually Assured Destruction). Join a rabble-rousing Catholic priest and Methodist minister, a kindergarten teacher, and a Quaker homemaker, as they beat swords into plowshares, or in this case, hammer on a B-52 bomber. Arrested and jailed, they bought the world time through doing time

Land of Deep Waters - Honduras, land of deep waters, a country torn apart by civil unrest, violence and poverty: Is it possible to go back? Thirty years after being banned from Honduras as a young nun, Joan, now married with two grown sons, finds herself haunted by memories of her four years there. She is determined to return, but how, and if so what will she find?

Still Dancing - Some phone calls we love, others we hate, like the ones Pastor Joe receives from his daughter's school. Or the one Dale received at work, letting him know his wife, Joy, had fallen and was in route to the hospital by ambulance. Could her cancer be back?

A Slow Waltz - The road to healing from loss is a slow one, sometimes going backward and sideways before going forward. Sometimes the biggest barrier to healing lies within us. Join Dale, Kathleen, Ava and others as they journey to forgiveness and healing.

Robertson also is author of four non-fiction books and writes two blogs each week. For more information about her books go to www.patriciamrobertson.com.

Still Dancing

Pastor Joe hated these phone calls most of all. As a minister he was used to all kinds of calls from church members in crisis from a tragic accident, runaway child or an arrest. Those he could handle. These he could not.

He pulled up to the high school, parked his car and walked the all-too-familiar path to the principal's office. Three calls in as many weeks. He was beginning to doubt his decision to enroll Stephanie in St. Luke's Lutheran high school.

"A new school for a new year. Time for a change," he had told his reluctant daughter.

He walked into the office, saw her slouched in a chair, her uniform skirt rolled up way above her knees.

He didn't say a word. Her attitude told him all he needed to know as they exchanged glances. Stephanie defiantly met his eyes as if to say, "See, I told you so." He refused to answer.

"Three detentions in three weeks," the principal stated calmly. "Perhaps St. Luke's is not the right environment for your daughter, Pastor. She clearly doesn't want to be here."

"What did she do this time?"

"Do you want the whole list or just the highlights?"

Pastor Joe paused to consider. "Just give it to me straight."

"Well, besides her general insubordination and refusal to participate in class, she's been caught smoking on school grounds again. In plain sight. It's as if she wants to be kicked out," she stated. "Are you sure this is the right place for her?"

Of course he wasn't sure. He wasn't sure about anything where Stephanie was concerned, but he couldn't tell the principal that. He was a church pastor, after all. He was supposed to know about these things. Why was it so easy to give out advice where his church members were concerned and so hard to accept it for his daughter?

"Let me talk to her."

"Fine. She has three days of detention. Maybe that will give you both time to think about what is best for Stephanie." Mrs. Clark paused before adding with concern in her voice. "I know you only want what is best for her. It's hard raising a daughter alone. Let me know if there is anything we can do to help. Perhaps the school counselor, Mrs. Deming, could help."

"Like I said, I'll talk to Stephanie and let you know."

It hadn't always been like this. Just six years ago she had been a happy eight-year-old, oblivious to any problems in the world as she lived in the supposedly perfect home with the supposedly perfect mom and dad. Then her world had been blown apart by the loss of her mom. Nothing had been the same since then.

Joe looked at his errant daughter and said, "Let's go," much as if he were commanding a puppy. Stephanie picked up her backpack and happily agreed, relieved to get out of the office.

"And roll your skirt back down to a proper length," he added. Again, Stephanie was only too happy to accommodate her father if it meant getting out of there quicker.

"Three days of detention," he mumbled at her as they walked to the car.

"I told you, Dad. They just have it in for me because I'm the minister's daughter – you know, a PK."

"I know about being a PK. You forget, I was one too, and I never got into the kinds of trouble you do. If it's such a problem for you, maybe you need to go to the public high school."

"Maybe I do," Stephanie said defiantly. "I've had enough of all of this phony religious, holier-than-thou freak show."

"Keep this up and you won't be welcome at that freak show. I could always send you to a boarding school."

"You're just looking for an excuse to get rid of me. I am just a problem since mom died, not like your precious Michelle. Why don't you ship both of us off to boarding school so you can bury yourself in your work – the way you always do – without feeling guilty about it."

"Keep up this attitude and I just may do that."

"Fine," Stephanie snapped as she threw her backpack into the car, climbing in the back seat.

"Fine," he responded, then added, "You know you can sit in the front."

"And talk to you? I'd rather die. I'll sit in the back like the prisoner I am."

"Fine," Joe repeated and started the car. That didn't go well, he thought to himself. Why did she provoke him like that? Why did he let himself be provoked? So like her mother and yet not like her. He didn't know what to do.

Despite the five years since his wife's death, he still felt like he was only half living, like he were in this state of limbo where he existed, nothing more. He who had helped so many grieving families had no ability to help his own. He had given up his position as pastor to a large congregation in an equally large city for a smaller congregation, all within one year of her death, something he had repeatedly told others not to do.

"Don't do anything drastic for the first year after a loss," he always advised. "Don't sell your home and move. Right now your home might feel like it is too painful to live in with the constant reminders of all you had lost, but a year from now those memories that haunt you may be precious reminders of your loved one."

He couldn't bear to live in that rectory with all of its memories, some good, more bad. He couldn't bear another casserole prepared by well-meaning church members and the single women in his church coming over, befriending his daughters, offering to help in the hope of winning him. Or even worse, the ones with pity in their eyes. He hated that he was now considered a desirable catch. He knew the lie of it. He was not a great catch.

A new start in a new town. That was what he had told himself he needed. Away from all the memories. A smaller congregation where no one knew him, with less responsibilities, a quiet town where he could raise his daughters in peace. Yes, there were still the single women, hoping to catch the new single man, but he ably rebuffed each of them, burying himself in his church work. He knew he didn't deserve love. He kept his distance behind a wall of his own making.

The girls had seemed to adapt to the move with little problem, at least at first. Stephanie had been ten at the time, Michelle seven. Both young enough to idolize their dad. But over time problems had started at school. Joe had been hopeful that the move from middle school to high school would have given Stephanie a chance to break out of the pattern she had established. Apparently not, as evidenced by the latest phone call.

Stephanie had stormed out of the car the minute he pulled into the driveway, heading into the house. Now would have been a good time to have another parent around, he thought, one who could head her off at the pass, stop her before she barricaded herself in her bedroom with music blaring. One who could play good cop to his bad cop. Now is when she could use a mother, but all she had was him.

"Wait, young lady. You're not going anywhere until I talk to you," he called after her.

She stopped in her tracks. "So talk," she said.

"Not here, wait till we get inside."

"Yes, that's right. We can't let any church member see that you have a less than perfect family." Now that had hurt. So much like her mother. Did she have any idea how much she was like her mother, he wondered. He followed her into the rectory, greeted the housekeeper then sat her down in the living room. He brushed his hand through his hair as he tried to figure out what to say. A woman's perspective would have been nice right then.

"So talk, Dad," Stephanie crossed her arms in front of her. Just then the phone rang. The housekeeper interrupted them.

"Pastor, it's for you. It sounds like an emergency."

Joe looked over at Stephanie and paused before saying, "I have to take this." He was quietly relieved at the reprieve from his parenting duties. "I'll be back in a minute."

"Sure you will, Dad. Take all of the time you need. You always do anyway. I'll be in my room," Stephanie said as she left the room.

Joe paused for just a minute, torn between his responsibilities as a parent and his responsibilities as a pastor. The pastor in him won out. After all, he knew what to do there.

"Pastor, it's Dale Reese. Can you come to the hospital? Something has happened to Joy."

"Is she all right?"

"We don't know. She collapsed while dancing. It appears to be a broken bone. We are waiting for x-ray results." Joe took down the necessary information.

"I'll be right there," he said, putting down the phone and giving instructions to the housekeeper before leaving.

"Stephanie, I'm going to the hospital. I'll talk to you when I get back." Stephanie didn't hear him as she listened to music through her head phones.

170

www.ingramcontent.com/pod-product-compliance
Lightning Source LLC
Chambersburg PA
CBHW070957120726
47910CB00004B/1269